P9-DXE-348

"TRANSPORTER ROOM," SPOCK SAID, "BEAM US UP—NOW."

"Do it!" Kirk confirmed instantly as he turned toward the science station.

"Yes, sir," Pritchard replied. "Transporters energizing . . . now. Just another second—"

Over the jumble of voices coming from Delkondros' headquarters there was the sizzling sound of an energy weapon. For an instant, it was louder on the communicator channel than were the voices, but then, abruptly, the communicator went dead.

"Laser fire!" Pritchard snapped, and then gasped. "Captain . . . both men—both lifeform readings— are gone! They must've been hit!"

Look for STAR TREK Fiction from Pocket Books

STAR TREK: The Original Series

STAR TREK: The Next Generation

STAR TREK®

RENEGADE

GENE DEWEESE

POCKET BOOKS

New York   London   Toronto   Sydney   Tokyo   Singapore

An *Original* Publication of POCKET BOOKS

POCKET BOOKS, a division of Simon & Schuster Inc.
1230 Avenue of the Americas, New York, NY 10020

ISBN: 0-671-65814-X

First Pocket Books printing June 1991

10 9 8 7 6 5 4 3 2 1

POCKET and colophon are registered trademarks of
Simon & Schuster Inc.

Printed in the U.S.A.

In memory of Fahf
1974–1991
As conscientious a cat as you'd ever want

Historian's Note

The events of *Renegade* take place during the last year of the *Enterprise's* original five-year mission.

Prologue

HARGEMON—he'd used the name so long, that was how he now thought of himself—looked up at his commander and laughed, the sound reverberating harshly in the cramped and spartan computer lab. "So, it will be *Enterprise* after all, with the *great* Captain James Tiberius Kirk in the hot seat!" The adjective dripped with sarcasm.

The commander smiled. "The luck of the draw. I thought you might be pleased."

"It couldn't happen to a better starship captain. He does so enjoy setting himself up as an example for others."

"You will, of course, need to alter your appearance, just in case."

"That would be necessary no matter what ship it was. All Starfleet officers pride themselves on their memories—among other less useful traits. But under the circumstances, it will require little more than what nature has already done." He grinned, brushing his

1

fingers across his full, but neatly trimmed, reddish-gray beard.

"*I* will decide what is required and what is not," the commander said, his smile abruptly disappearing. "I will not allow half measures, not in this. There is far too much at stake. Far too many people have worked far too hard to allow one individual to jeopardize that work because of carelessness. Or," he added, eyes narrowing in warning, "because of ego or because of any personal agenda that individual might consider pursuing."

"Don't worry," Hargemon snapped. "I am as aware of the importance of our objective as you!" He waved his hands at the racks of equipment that crammed the tiny lab. "Don't forget, I'm the one who's put in thousands of hours on these primitive devices you call computers! I am also aware that without me—"

"Without you, my objective cannot be accomplished. Yes, I am well aware of how important your talents are. I found and recruited you, after all. But in the event of failure, I will be forced to reconsider my initial judgment. Just remember: *I* will have a second chance. *You* will not. Now go, prepare. I will inspect the results when you have finished."

"I do not need—"

"I will inspect the results when you have finished," the commander repeated, his voice icy as he turned his back on Hargemon and pushed out through the plain metal door that was the room's only exit.

The self-righteous bastard! Hargemon seethed. *He's*

getting to be as much of a tyrant as Kirk! But he said nothing, only glowered at the door as it clicked shut. Turning back to the control console, he sucked in a deep, calming breath. Once Kirk was taken care of, there would be plenty of time for the "commander" and the rest—plenty of time and opportunity.

Chapter One

Captain's Log, Supplemental:

We are en route to the planet Chyrellka to do—as Dr. McCoy might put it—a little fire-fighting.

We first made contact with the Chyrellkans ten years ago. They declined membership in the Federation, but at the time of that initial encounter, Captain Brittany Mendez of the *Exeter* noted that the Chyrellkans and their colony on Vancadia provided a textbook example of how to peacefully establish and administer a colony.

Unlike most emerging technological civilizations, the Chyrellkans had established a working world government before leaving their own atmosphere. And once their probes showed them that Vancadia's biosphere was almost identical to their own—except for the absence of any lifeforms higher than tree-dwelling primates—they went about establishing a colony with Vulcan-like logic and determination.

Without impulse drive technology, all early trips to Vancadia were one-way. Shuttles lifted them into orbit around Chyrellka, where they transferred to orbital-built interplanetary ships. At Vancadia, then, they descended from orbit in one-way landers. It was nearly forty years before the colonials reached the stage at which they could manufacture the boosters that allowed them to return to orbit.

From the beginning, the Chyrellkans had planned for the

Vancadian colonists to be given their independence once they'd achieved total self-sufficiency. A decade ago, Captain Mendez noted that with Vancadia's population close to eight million, the goal of self-sufficiency seemed only a few years away.

And yet now the Federation has received an urgent request for help in mediating what the Chyrellkan message describes as "an increasingly vicious dispute between Chyrellka and her rebelling colony."

HIS PALE SKIN accentuated by a jet-black helmet of tightly curling hair and an equally dark, carefully sculpted beard, the Chyrellkan leader's face loomed large on the *Enterprise* viewscreen. Other faces, out of focus, were dimly visible in the background.

"Welcome to Chyrellkan space," the leader said. "I am Kaulidren. My people and I appreciate the promptness with which your Federation has responded to our request."

"Thank you, Kaulidren," Kirk said. "Premier Kaulidren, is it?"

The head inclined in an almost imperceptible nod of acknowledgment. "And you are Captain James Kirk, commanding the U.S.S. *Enterprise.* Am I right?"

"You are, Premier. We will be entering orbit in a few minutes and will be ready to beam you and your party aboard as soon as the *Enterprise* matches orbits with your ship."

"That is most kind of you, Captain," Kaulidren said, holding up one hand, palm out, "but no, thank you. Consider it superstition if you wish, but it is disquieting to me, this prospect of having my component atoms disassembled and transmitted unprotected through space in the hope that they can be fitted back together in your transporter room."

"I wouldn't consider it superstition at all, Premier," Kirk said, suppressing a smile as he saw Dr. McCoy, safely off screen, give a quick grimace of agreement with Kaulidren. "I assure you, however, that the transporter is perfectly safe. But if you prefer—"

"I do prefer, Captain, particularly since it is my understanding that your vessel is easily capable of receiving my entire ship. I trust I have not been misled."

"Not at all, Premier. Your ship is somewhat larger than our own shuttlecraft, but the hangar deck will accommodate it easily. Our landing tractor beams can handle—"

"I would prefer to bring my ship in under its own power, if that is possible."

Kirk suppressed a frown. "It's possible, yes, but I understand that your ship is powered by conventional rocket engines. It would be dangerous to use them in any enclosed area, even one as large as the hangar deck."

"My ship is equipped with maneuvering jets— which would surely pose no threat—and are fully adequate for docking maneuvers in space."

"In zero gravity, yes, Premier, but in the hangar deck, as in all parts of the *Enterprise*, a constant one-g is maintained."

Premier Kaulidren was silent a moment. "Artificial

gravity," he said finally. "I had forgotten. But is it not possible to temporarily remove the gravity from individual areas?"

"It would be easier to use the landing tractor beams." *Or the transporter system,* Kirk added silently.

"But it is possible? Without causing major disruptions to your ship?"

"It's possible, yes." *No point in arguing,* Kirk thought. *Save it for things that count, like getting the Premier and his opposite number among the colonists to start talking to each other.* "I will make the necessary arrangements."

"Thank you, Captain. I look forward to our meeting face to face and to a discussion of our problems."

Abruptly, the screen went blank.

"They've ceased transmission, sir," Lieutenant Uhura volunteered. "Shall I try to get them back?"

"Not for now, Lieutenant. Mr. Sulu, how long till rendezvous?"

"Just under five minutes, Captain."

Kirk tapped a button on the arm of the command chair. "Mr. Scott? You heard?"

"Aye, Captain, I heard. I canna' say I approve, but I heard."

"I'm on your side, Scotty, but let's go along with the Premier on the small things. Unless I miss my guess, there'll be more than enough bigger ones coming along."

"Aye, Captain, I know what ye're saying. The

hangar deck will be zero gravity when the doors open. I trust ye'll warn any affected personnel. Two o' my lads are in the shuttlecraft bay, checking—"

"I'll leave that honor to you, Mr. Scott," Kirk said, standing up from the command chair and heading for the turbolift. "Mr. Spock, Dr. McCoy? From the sound of the Premier, he will expect to be met by nothing less than our most senior officers."

Ten minutes later the three stood looking down on the hangar deck from the rear observation gallery— Scotty had been able to retain normal gravity in the rear third of the deck—as the Chyrellkan ship slowly drifted in through the open hangar doors. Guided by minute pulses from its maneuvering jets, the incoming ship reminded Kirk of nothing more than a small, sleek version of the original United States space shuttles, still kept clean and glistening in the Spaceflight Museum. Even the insignia—seven 7-pointed stars on a diagonally striped red-and-green background—was not all that different.

As the ship cleared the faintly shimmering atmospheric containment field, the doors began to clamshell shut.

But the ship continued to drift forward, its pilot either missing or ignoring the landing target painted on the deck.

"What the blazes is he up to?" McCoy muttered as the ship drifted between the deck operations control towers, toward the shuttle elevator. "If he gets back here where the gravity is still on—"

"Don't worry, Bones," Kirk said, glancing up at the two ensigns standing by the controls of the landing tractor beams. "We're ready, if it comes to that."

But it didn't—quite. Seconds before Kirk decided it was time to signal the ensigns to take over the landing, the forward maneuvering jets finally came to life and cancelled the forward motion.

However, the ship was still moving, Kirk realized a moment later, but now it was going sideways. Frowning, he again started to signal the ensigns, but before he could complete the motion, a final series of puffs brought the ship to a stop, one sharp-pointed wing almost touching the wall beneath the forward observation gallery walkway. With only the faintest of thumps and creaks, it settled to the deck on its extended landing gear, its tires bulging slightly as Scotty restored gravity a moment after touchdown.

Even as Kirk and the others started down the steps from the walkway to the hangar floor, one of the ship's doors retracted inward and slid smoothly to one side. A set of steps descended from the opening, and Kaulidren stepped out of the shadowy interior. Clad in a dark gray, not-quite-military uniform, he stood watching silently as the three officers approached. When they were in position, he quickly moved down the steps, pointedly avoiding touching the handrails to steady himself, as if to prove that he had taken the abrupt transition from zero to one-g in stride. The clean-shaven four who emerged after him, wearing similar but lighter uniforms, were less quick to adapt, gripping the metal handrails with each step. One, carrying a metallic, briefcase-like container with what looked like an old-fashioned keypad lock, almost lost his footing on the first step.

"Welcome aboard the *Enterprise,* Premier Kaulidren," Kirk said, momentarily lowering his head in the fractional bow that his briefing had indicated was the proper form of greeting. Kaulidren, however, instead of returning the bow, stepped forward and extended his hand.

"We are on a Federation ship," he said flatly. "We will observe Federation customs."

It's Federation custom to use transporters, Kirk thought, but kept a smile on his face as he took the Premier's hand. The grip, he discovered, was as firm and practiced as any admiral's. The other four dutifully offered their hands as Kaulidren introduced them collectively and anonymously as his "advisors," but their grips were tentative, even uneasy.

"My first officer, Commander Spock," Kirk said when the last of the four had shuttled backward to flank Kaulidren, "and my chief medical officer, Lieutenant Commander Leonard McCoy."

Kaulidren extended his hand to each in turn but then turned back to Spock. "Vulcan, if I am not mistaken, Commander."

"That is correct, Premier," Spock acknowledged.

"That is good," Kaulidren said, nodding. "I understand Vulcans are known for their logic and impartiality."

"They are," Kirk agreed, ignoring the beginnings of a puzzled frown on McCoy's face. "You are remarkably well informed, Premier."

"Even though we have chosen to remain independent of your Federation, we have tried to absorb whatever information you have offered to share with us. In any event, I am encouraged by Commander Spock's presence. Those qualities of logic and impartiality will be much in need if we are to resolve our current difficulties."

"I will, of course, assist in any way I can, Premier," Spock said.

"That goes without saying," Kaulidren said, turning back to Kirk. "Now, I have been told that your computers—Duotronic, I believe they are called—are capable of accepting information generated by our own comparatively primitive systems."

"In all probability, yes," Kirk said. "Duotronics, as I'm sure you know, are remarkably versatile."

"Yes," Kaulidren said, looking around the hangar deck, "it is my understanding that they literally run the entire ship."

"Supervised by the crew," McCoy put in.

"Of course. After all, computers are mere machines, no matter how complex. They require constant human supervision. At least, that is the case with our own, and I assume it is still the case even with yours."

"Absolutely," McCoy said emphatically enough to minutely arch Spock's eyebrow and draw a flickering sideways glance from Kirk.

"Very well." Kaulidren gestured at the briefcase-like box still held by one of his advisors. "I have with me records documenting a small portion of the atrocities the rebel terrorists have committed. I trust your computer will be able to verify their authenticity."

"It will be able to verify that the events recorded were actual events, not computer-generated images," Spock said, "but that is all. As for the identities and affiliations of the individuals involved, no such authentication is possible. In such matters we must rely solely on your words, Premier."

"Are you suggesting—" Kaulidren began, scowling.

"I was suggesting nothing, Premier. I was simply stating a fact."

The scowl was gone as quickly as it had come. "Of course. My apologies, Commander Spock. I'm afraid my dealings with the rebels—some of whom I once considered my friends—have made me quick to mistrust. I ask only that you look at what I have to show you, and listen to what I have to say."

Pulling in a breath, Kaulidren turned to look over his shoulder at the ship. A sixth man—this one inches taller than Kaulidren or any of the others, and wearing a darker shade of uniform with a sidearm of some kind strapped to its belt—had emerged from the ship and was standing stiffly at the top of the steps just outside the door, which now eased itself shut.

"I hope you will not be offended, Captain, if one of my men remains on post while we are away from our ship."

"Of course not," Kirk said, suppressing a frown, "but I assure you it isn't necessary."

"I understand. However, irrational as it may be, I would feel more comfortable with him there."

"As you wish, Premier. Now, if you will come with us, we can get down to business." *For all the good it will do,* Kirk added skeptically to himself as he led the way to the elevators, *if you don't trust us any more than that.*

Minutes later they were settling into chairs around the briefing room table while Spock inserted Kaulidren's data tapes into the computer. The control panel lights flickered as the computer began to analyze the Chyrellkan devices and adapt its own input circuitry to read the data.

"As I understand it, Premier," Kirk said as they waited for the still-blank computer screen to light up, "Vancadia was scheduled to be given its independence only two years from now, on the one-hundredth anniversary of Chyrellka's first landing there."

Kaulidren snorted. "Perfectly true. But they weren't content to wait."

"But according to Starfleet records, there was no sign of trouble when your worlds were first contacted. None that our representatives could detect, at any rate."

"There *was* no trouble—then."

"But now there obviously is. What happened in the meantime, Premier? How did the relationship between your worlds deteriorate so rapidly?"

Kaulidren gestured sharply at the slot into which Spock had inserted the data. "It's all there—the terrorism, the killings, the destruction."

"I understand," Kirk persisted, "but does it explain how it started? *Why* it started? There have to be reasons, and if we're to be of any help, we have to find them."

Kaulidren frowned, then shrugged. "If you speak with the 'rebels,' perhaps *they* will be able to explain. It is a total mystery to me. As you say, Vancadia was scheduled to be *given* its independence only two years from now. But three years ago they apparently decided they needed it immediately. Their spokesman was a fire-breather named Delkondros."

"Did they give any reasons for their sudden . . . impatience?"

Kaulidren shrugged. "I can only assume that they grew tired of waiting. Or that Delkondros convinced them there was no need to wait. He was only one of twenty Council members at the time, but very ambitious," he added with a grimace. "Or, to give him the benefit of the doubt, very opportunistic. In either case, within weeks after he became President of the Council he began beating the drums for instant independence and making outrageous accusations about our colonial administrators. But then he turned openly to violence, although several of the more rational members of the Council repudiated him. There was no reasoning with him, and in the end, we had no choice but to declare him and the Council members who remained with him outlaws. They went into hiding and have conducted a terrorist campaign against us ever since."

Kaulidren broke off, looking impatiently toward Spock and the computer.

"The data is being processed, Captain," Spock volunteered. "It does appear to be genuine."

Kaulidren snorted. "Of course it is genuine! Do you think we are such fools that we would try to trick a Starfleet computer? Now, can the data be displayed?"

Spock swiveled the screen so it faced the others at the table. A frozen image appeared: the interior of a small room with one cluttered desk, a pair of wooden chairs, and several old-fashioned file cabinets. The camera had apparently been mounted high on one of the walls. A graying man in a dark, loose-cut tunic and trousers sat behind the desk, his back to a large window. A younger man in a lighter tunic stood facing him, leaning forward, both hands on the desktop. Both were studying some papers atop the clutter of other papers. For the first few seconds the image was grainy and ill-defined, but the focus sharpened instant by instant.

"Is something wrong?" Kaulidren asked sharply. "Why is nothing moving?"

"More processing," Kirk explained. "The computer is staying with the first frame while it cleans up the images. As soon as—"

The image began moving and speaking.

"I see," Kaulidren said, motioning for the sound to be turned down. "This is the first 'incident' we have a

16

direct record of. A half-dozen attacks were made before we put all our offices under constant camera surveillance. The man behind the desk is—was—our chief administrator for the northwest colonial district. The other was his assistant, a colonial himself, but apparently he was considered an enemy for associating with us. Or simply expendable."

Swallowing, Kaulidren averted his eyes. "I have seen this 'incident' all too often already, Captain Kirk. Your computer's 'cleaning up' can only make it all the more disquieting."

On the screen, the two men continued to talk silently. Suddenly, the window behind the desk shattered. Before either man could react, shards of glass sprayed the room, and a package the size and shape of a large brick thudded against the back of the man behind the desk. For a split second both men started to look toward the object, the man behind the desk simultaneously grimacing in pain.

But then, with neither of them having actually seen the object, both jerked about and started to flee.

But only started. The man in front of the desk completed his turn and took a single, lurching stride toward the door. Simultaneously, the one behind the desk jerked erect, slamming the chair backward, and began a leap that would have taken him to the top of the desk.

Then the explosion came.

It was over in an instant, the body of the man behind the desk barely beginning a head-over-heels arc upward, when the lens of the camera was shattered as something—a piece of the chair from behind the desk?—smashed into it. Moments later a new picture appeared, this one taken from the hall outside the shattered room as a half dozen would-be rescue workers uncovered the bodies in the rubble of the shattered desk and the partially collapsed walls and ceiling.

"You see," Kaulidren said, returning his eyes briefly to the screen, "that is typical of the rebel butchery. There were no warnings—unless you consider their earlier murders to be warnings of all the subsequent murders. Those two men—both friends of mine, I might add—were given no chance to escape. They were simply executed."

"Is the rest of the 'information' you've brought us similar to this?" Kirk asked flatly.

"It is documentation of the brutality of the rebels, yes."

"And nothing else?"

"If you doubt the authenticity—"

"There is no doubt of the authenticity of the events themselves," Kirk said, "but as Mr. Spock has already pointed out, there is no way to verify who the victims were or who their killers were. And even if there were, that would not change the basic fact that such happenings, no matter how barbaric, will do nothing to help us accomplish our objective. What we need are—"

"But this *shows* you what kind of people we are dealing with! Certainly you can see that!"

Kirk suppressed a sigh that was a mixture of sympathy and irritation. "Premier Kaulidren," he said, "we are here, at your government's request, to attempt to mediate a peace between yourself and the rebels. The first step toward that goal is for us to find the underlying cause of the conflict."

"But we thought, once you were aware of the facts—"

"That the Federation would take your side in the dispute?"

Kaulidren blinked, apparently taken aback at Kirk's directness. He pulled in a breath. "Surely you would not take the side of murderers and terrorists!"

"Premier Kaulidren—" Kirk spread his hands before him on the table in a gesture of supplication. "Please understand—we are not here to take sides at all. Our prime directive does not *allow* us to take sides. We are here to learn as much of the truth as we can, and to use that knowledge in an effort to end the hostilities."

"But Captain Kirk—"

"Captain," Uhura's voice broke in on the intercom, "incoming transmission from Vancadia."

Kirk glanced at Kaulidren, who was frowning at the interruption. "Patch it through, Lieutenant," he said.

"Right away, sir."

A moment later her voice was replaced by an angry male voice. "—Kaulidren's self-serving lies!" it began, obviously in the middle of a sentence.

"I am not lying!" Kaulidren exploded, drowning out the next few words before Kirk waved him to silence.

"—before it is too late!" The voice finished and then paused.

"It's a recording, sir," Uhura said quickly. "Stand by for repeat."

"You must not listen to Kaulidren!" the voice began without preamble. "No matter what lies he has told you about our so-called terrorism, I represent the colonists, and if your Federation is truly committed to justice, you must speak with *us* before you take any action. You must come to Vancadia and learn the truth about Kaulidren's self-serving lies! You must hear us, before it is too late!"

"Have you located the source, Lieutenant?" Kirk asked.

"Lieutenant Pritchard is doing a sensor scan, Captain."

"Lieutenant Pritchard?" Kirk addressed the young officer manning the science station while Spock was off the bridge.

"Yes, sir, I have it. The message is coming from a small ship launched from the surface of Vancadia a few minutes ago. It is still under power and is about to enter orbit."

"Lieutenant Uhura, try to establish communication."

"Already trying, sir, but it is not a subspace message. At this distance, it will be at least three minutes before any response is possible."

"Understood, Lieutenant. Keep trying. We'll move closer." Kirk turned to Kaulidren. "If you wish, we will delay our departure until you and your men can return to your ship."

"What?" Kaulidren exploded. "You are leaving?

Captain, surely you are not going to meet with those butchers!"

Kirk nodded crisply. "We will indeed be proceeding to Vancadia, Premier. If you wish to remain aboard, you are welcome. If not—"

"Of course I will remain! There's no telling what new lies they have concocted!"

"Very well, Premier." Speaking again to the intercom, Kirk stood up. "We're on our way to the bridge. Lieutenant Sulu, lay in a course to Vancadia."

"But there is more data—" Kaulidren began, gesturing angrily at the computer screen, now blank.

"It will still be there when we reach Vancadia, Premier."

"As you wish, Captain, but—"

"Captain!" Lieutenant Pritchard interrupted. "The ship transmitting that message—it's been destroyed!"

Chapter Two

"DETAILS, MR. PRITCHARD," Kirk snapped, pausing over the intercom while glancing sharply at Kaulidren and his retinue. Their faces, however, were unreadable.

"There were a dozen much larger ships already in orbit around Vancadia," Pritchard reported. "Two of them fired almost simultaneously on the message ship just as it was entering orbit. It had been transmitting continuously from the moment it left the planet's atmosphere."

"Survivors?"

"It was too distant for the sensors to detect survivors, sir, or how many, if any, lifeforms were on board before the attack. Tentative mass readings indicated a craft too small to accommodate more than two individuals."

"Very well. Mr. Sulu, get us under way, full impulse power."

"Aye-aye, sir."

Kirk shut off the intercom. "Gentlemen, if you'll

come with me to the bridge . . ." He led the way to the nearest turbolift, Kaulidren and his retinue directly behind, with Spock and McCoy to the rear.

"What do you know about what happened, Premier?" he asked as the door hissed shut behind them. "You don't seem all that surprised."

"I am not, Captain. I assume that one of our surveillance ships was responsible."

"Surveillance ships?"

"We maintain a constant watch on Vancadia. Their attempts to bring their terrorist activities to Chyrellka itself have made it essential."

"Shooting down an unarmed ship does not constitute surveillance, Premier," Spock pointed out.

Before Kaulidren could answer, the doors opened on the bridge. Vancadia already filled the forward screen.

"Reducing to quarter impulse power, Captain," Sulu reported. "Entering standard orbit about Vancadia."

Kaulidren's eyes widened as he followed Kirk onto the bridge. "We have reached Vancadia so soon?"

"For an interstellar ship, Premier, interplanetary distances are short. Mr. Pritchard, any indication of survivors, now that we're within sensor range?"

"None, sir." Looking up, Pritchard saw Spock and stepped back, relinquishing his position at the science station as he completed his report. "But neither is there any indication that the ship contained any lifeforms before the attack. Analysis of the debris mass lowers our previous estimates of vessel size. It could have contained no more than a single individual and was more likely unmanned and remote-controlled."

"If anyone was aboard, Captain," Uhura volunteered, "there *was* time for them to have received our reply before the destruction, but there was no acknowledgment. The same signal kept repeating until the end."

"You're positive there was enough time, Lieutenant?"

"Yes, sir. The destruction was approximately one minute after our signals would have reached them."

Which doesn't prove anything, Kirk thought grimly. With the surveillance ships attacking, a lone pilot would have had other things on his mind.

Turning his attention to the forward viewing screen, he saw that a ship, presumably a Chyrellkan surveillance ship, was hovering in the distance. Hundreds of times the size of the sleek ship on the hangar deck, its blocky form was obviously designed never to descend into a planet's atmosphere. Laser ports dotted its rectangular prow like deadly, geometrically perfect freckles.

"That's a formidable ship, Premier," Kirk observed, turning to Kaulidren. "Will we need our shields?"

Kaulidren looked shocked. "I would not want this to be divulged to the Vancadians," he said, stepping down into the command area of the bridge to stand next to Kirk, "but all but three of the laser ports are dummies, and much of the bulk is empty space. We have learned that the more formidable a weapon appears to be, the less chance there is that it will ever have to be used."

"But this one has obviously been used, Premier," Kirk persisted. "We just *saw* it being used. And lasers of that power—even if there are only three, rather than twenty-three—can still be deadly to an unprotected ship. I ask you again, will we need our shields?"

"Not for protection against *us*, certainly," Kaulidren said indignantly.

"But for protection against the rebels? Is that what you're implying?"

"They would try anything."

"The ship you just shot down—what was it 'trying'?" McCoy broke in.

"Gentlemen, you have to understand the situation we are confronted with," Kaulidren said earnestly. "If we were to allow them unhindered access to space—"

"Captain," Uhura said, "electromagnetic signal from the planet's surface coming in. No visual."

"On speakers, Lieutenant, and patch it through to engineering. Mr. Scott, are you there?"

"Aye, Captain," Scotty's voice came over the intercom.

A moment later another voice filled the bridge, the same voice they had heard from the downed ship. "Calling Federation starship," it began, more anxious than angry this time, and apparently not a recording, "can you hear me?"

"We can hear you," Kirk replied. "This is Captain James Kirk, commanding the U.S.S. *Enterprise*. Identify yourself."

A jumble of other voices erupted briefly from the radio, but then the original one returned, now speaking calmly, even deliberately. "I am Delkondros, President of the Vancadian Independence Council. In the wanton and unprovoked destruction of our ship, you have seen the true face of the Chyrellkan tyrants! If—"

"You *knew* it would be shot down!" Kaulidren broke in angrily. "You sent it up to *be* shot down!"

"Kaulidren?" The stilted formality vanished from Delkondros' voice, replaced by a cold fury. "What lies did you tell to be allowed aboard a Federation ship?"

"Ask him!" Kaulidren demanded. "Ask him why he sent up a ship he *knew* would be shot down!"

"And ask *him,*" Delkondros shot back, "why it *was* shot down! There was no warning, simply a vicious, unprovoked attack. Your robot killers did not know if there was a crew on board or not! They *never* know! And *you* do not *care!*"

"And who made the *first* attack?" Kaulidren was shouting now. "Who would have killed thousands if they hadn't been stopped? Do not blame Chyrellka for the results of *your* madness, Delkondros!"

"Gentlemen!" Kirk broke in sharply. "We are here to mediate, not to referee."

"But you saw what Kaulidren's forces did to our ship!" the voice protested.

"We saw," Kirk said. "We have also seen records of what the Premier claims the Vancadians have done."

"Lies! All lies! If you want the truth, you must come here, to Vancadia! We have true *evidence*—the bodies of our assassinated leaders! If your medical science is as great as we are led to believe, you will find the Chyrellkan poisons still in their tissues!"

"Don't listen to him!" Kaulidren broke in. "Even if such poisons exist, they are *his* doing, not ours! Ask him how he came to be elected to the Council in the first place, how his opponent conveniently died the very week before the election!"

"My opponent *'died,'* Premier Kaulidren, because you thought *I* would be easier to control, easier to make a fool of! But you were wrong! And when you realized your mistake, you had your puppets in the Colonial Administration try to kill *me,* and when that didn't work, you tried to kill our entire government!"

"You killed your government when you became terrorists, when you began killing us!"

"Gentlemen, please!" Kirk snapped, suddenly impatient. He had briefly hoped that by simply letting the two go at each other, he could listen and gain some insight into the situation, but that was obviously not going to happen. "Screaming accusations at each other is not going to help. Now unless either of you has something more than a recitation of atrocities allegedly committed by the other side—"

"Very well, Captain Kirk!" Delkondros broke in harshly. "If you doubt my word, send someone down!

Send a *physician* down! Let him look at the evidence, let him examine those of us who have survived the slaughter! Let *him* decide who is telling the truth! Perhaps he could even find the *source* of the poisons! Or provide the antidote that Kaulidren refuses to share with us!"

Kirk cast a questioning glance toward McCoy. "Bones?"

"You think you have to *ask*, Jim?" McCoy said, heading for the turbolift. "I'll be ready as soon as I get my tricorder and medikit."

Kirk smiled faintly. "If you wish, President Delkondros, our ship's physician can beam down and . . . evaluate your evidence. He can also determine if an antidote to the poison exists or can be synthesized. Will that be satisfactory?"

"Of course it will! All we want is an honest investigation that will lead to the truth! And save lives!"

"And the Vulcan!" Kaulidren interjected. "Ask Delkondros if he will accept an observer who will be influenced only by logic, not by cheap emotional theatrics."

"There is a Vulcan on board?" Delkondros's voice crackled back, not quite drowning out the amused snort that came from the turbolift as the doors closed behind McCoy.

"My first officer, Mr. Spock, is half Vulcan," Kirk said mildly.

"Then of course we would welcome him," Delkondros said. "We have nothing to fear from logic or impartiality. On the contrary, we have great need of those qualities!"

Kaulidren scowled but said nothing.

"Mr. Spock?" Kirk turned toward the science station. "Would you care to join the doctor and me?"

"Of course, Captain."

"Captain!" Kaulidren frowned. "Surely you are not going *with* them!"

Unable to suppress his own frown this time, Kirk turned to Kaulidren. "I thought I might go along for the ride, Premier. Is there some reason I shouldn't?"

"Undoubtedly he fears for your safety, Captain," Delkondros' voice cut in, now edged with sarcasm rather than anger. "But to tell the truth, I, too, would prefer you remain aboard your ship—where you can keep an eye on the Premier. I would certainly not trust him—"

"As you wish, gentlemen," Kirk said, his own voice reflecting some of the President's sarcasm. "Far be it from me to deny the two of you virtually the first thing you've agreed on since our arrival. President Delkondros, I'll have you connected directly to the transporter room. You can give the officer in charge the coordinates for beam-down." Kirk nodded to Uhura, who toggled a switch on her console. "Now, Premier Kaulidren—"

"Captain Kirk," Kaulidren said, "I strongly advise against sending your men down there."

Frowning, Kirk turned back to the Chyrellkan. "And why is that, Premier? A few moments ago you seemed willing—even eager—for Spock, at least, to go."

"I never thought for a second Delkondros would accept! But now that he has, I realize it must be a trap. You have not dealt with these people, Captain. You do not know them, don't know what they're capable of. Please—you must view the remainder of the data I brought aboard before you decide to deliver your men into Delkondros's hands."

Kirk shook his head. "The rebels have to realize that any action they might take against my men would be totally counterproductive."

"They are completely irrational!" Kaulidren sputtered. Kirk caught Spock's eye and could tell his first officer's thoughts echoed his own: *Now there's the pot calling the kettle black.* He would have laughed if the situation wasn't so clearly desperate. "Premier," Kirk began—but before he could continue, the computer's feminine voice cut him off.

"Intruder alert," it said, emotionless as always. "Unauthorized personnel have been detected in the main computer room on deck eight."

Chapter Three

SPINNING TOWARD the main viewscreen, Kirk flicked his eyes across Kaulidren's men. None were missing.

"Computer," he snapped, stabbing a button on the arm of the command chair, "seal access doors to main computer room. Security, send a detail to the main computer room, deck eight. Intruder alert."

"Security, aye, sir," Lieutenant Shanti's slightly accented contralto voice acknowledged almost instantly.

"Mr. Spock, get the computer room on the screen."

"Trying, Captain," Spock said, not looking up. "Control circuits are not responding."

"Computer," Kirk said, a sense of unease gnawing at him, "identify intruder."

"Unknown humanoid," it began, then fell silent.

"Computer?"

The machine remained silent.

Kirk darted a glance at Spock, still working at the science station controls. "Are the access doors sealed?"

"Indications are contradictory, Captain."

Kirk crossed the bridge quickly to stand next to his first officer. "Override, Mr. Spock!"

The Vulcan shook his head. "Not possible under these conditions, Captain. None of the controls are—"

Spock broke off. A moment later the cramped aisles of the main computer room appeared on the viewscreen. They were empty. The access doors, sealed as the image appeared, slid quietly open a moment later.

"The monitor circuit malfunction," the computer's monotone announced, "has been isolated and corrected."

"Monitor circuit malfunction?" Kirk asked sharply. He turned to Spock.

"I believe, Captain, that the computer is saying that the alert was the result of a malfunction."

"Affirmative," the computer replied instantly.

"There was no one in the main computer room?" Kirk asked.

"Affirmative."

Kirk frowned. "Lieutenant Shanti, status report."

"Exiting turbolift on deck eight, Captain, proceeding to main computer room."

"The alert may have been a false alarm, Lieutenant, but be careful anyway. Report anything the least bit unusual."

"Yes, sir."

"Mr. Spock, any indication of the cause of the malfunction?"

"None, Captain. Readings indicate only that there was a conflict between two different sets of sensors within the room. The computer's efforts to reconcile the conflict appears to have resulted in the temporary lockup of the control circuits and at least the partial erasure of the conflicting readings."

Dr. McCoy would say that sounded like a nervous breakdown, Kirk thought. "What, specifically, was the conflict, Mr. Spock?"

"Unknown, Captain. Given time, a complete diagnostic program could be run, but because of the apparent erasures there is less than a ten-point-seven percent chance that a specific cause could be isolated. There is also a special program I have been devising that could increase those odds an indeterminate amount, but it is as yet untested."

Kirk nodded, turning back to the main viewscreen. "Do what you can, Mr. Spock."

"Of course, Captain."

"Captain," Lieutenant Shanti's voice came over the intercom, "the computer room is empty and all appears in order. However, one of my men reports having heard the turbolift operate."

"Computer," Kirk snapped, "image of turbolift interior."

The viewscreen shimmered uncharacteristically for a moment as the computer room vanished and was replaced by the interior of the turbolift. It was empty, its doors just closing, giving the bridge crew a brief glimpse of the hangar deck, with the Chyrellkan shuttle in the distance.

"Computer," Kirk ordered, "show the hangar deck. Lieutenant Shanti, proceed to hangar deck immediately."

"Yes, sir."

On the forward viewscreen, the hangar deck appeared. Kaulidren's ship looked the same as it had in the glimpse through the turbolift door. The massive guard still stood impassively at the top of the steps, his eyes calmly and deliberately scanning the deserted expanse of the deck. To one side were the parked shuttlecraft, except for the one Scott's men were working on in the deck twenty maintenance shop. The tractor beam control room high along one wall was empty, the two ensigns Kirk had placed there temporarily having returned to their regular duties.

From somewhere came a sound, a faint scrape of metal on metal, but it was immediately obscured by the hiss of the turbolift doors. Lieutenant Shanti stepped out, her diminutive frame dwarfed by the two husky six-footers comprising her security detail. Her size was deceptive, however: Kirk knew that, with her martial arts skills, she could hold her own with either of them.

"Lieutenant Shanti," he began but was interrupted by Kaulidren, who had remained uncharacteristically quiet during the alert.

"What is happening, Captain Kirk? Why have you sent these people to my ship?"

"Lieutenant Shanti," Kirk repeated over Kaulidren's words, "there was a metallic sound somewhere in the hangar deck just as you arrived. Can you see anything that might account for it?"

"We heard it too, Captain," she said, "just as the doors were opening. It seemed to come from the vicinity of the alien ship."

"I see." Kirk darted another glance at Kaulidren as he turned toward the science station. "Mr. Spock, scan the hangar deck for lifeforms."

Spock concentrated on the station readouts for a moment. "Only the security detail and the Premier's sentry register, Captain."

Kirk turned back to the image of the hangar deck, watching it silently for several seconds. "Lieutenant Shanti," he said finally, "return to the main computer room. Check it out thoroughly for any indication that the malfunction wasn't a malfunction."

"Yes, sir," Shanti acknowledged. "For evidence of a real intruder, you mean, sir?"

"Correct, Lieutenant."

"Captain Kirk," Kaulidren spoke up abruptly, "are you saying there might actually have been someone in your computer room?"

"I can't overlook any possibility, Premier."

"Someone in the computer room—would such a person have had access to computers everywhere in your ship from that one room?"

"Of course. Why?"

"The data I brought aboard, which your first officer placed in the briefing room computer—could that have been . . . affected by this hypothetical intruder?"

Kirk suppressed a frown and an impulse to point out to the Premier that if there really had been an intruder, all indications were that he had come aboard in the Premier's own shuttle.

"If an intruder existed," he said evenly, "if he knew precisely what he was looking for, *and* if he had an encyclopedic knowledge of the computer as well as an extraordinary skill in making use of that knowledge, then it would be remotely possible. At a conservative estimate, however, there are no more than two or three dozen people with that kind of computer expertise in all of Starfleet."

"And none are aboard the *Enterprise?*"

"Only one, Premier, and I assure you he was nowhere near the computer room at the time of the malfunction."

"How can you be so positive, Captain?"

"For the same reason you can be, Premier. Mr. Spock hasn't been out of sight of either of us since you came aboard."

Kaulidren darted a glance toward Spock, then seemed to relax. "Of course, Captain, my apologies. These last few months it's hard not to become at least a little paranoid. But for me to entertain even for a moment the thought that my enemies could have gained such knowledge and then found their way aboard a Federation starship just so they could tamper with my data is beyond even my worst paranoid fantasies. Again, my apologies. However, regarding the decision to allow your people to beam down to—"

As if on cue, the turbolift door hissed open and Dr. McCoy emerged and glanced around. "I see you and my Vulcan logical half are still loitering up here. Does this mean you've been talked out of it and I'll be going down by myself?"

"We had a false alarm in the computer room," Kirk explained, "but it's under control now. Correct, Mr. Spock?"

"All readings now appear normal, Captain, but . . ." a crease furrowed Spock's brow, "I have not been able to determine the precise cause or nature of the malfunction."

There was a snort of laughter from the doctor. "Did I hear you right, Spock? Did you just admit there was something you *couldn't* do? And with the computer, no less? Sorry I missed it. Now, are you ready to go, or do I beam down by myself?"

"Spock is ready, Bones," Kirk said, grimacing faintly as he gestured for Lieutenant Pritchard to return to the science station, "but I'll be staying on board, at the request of our guest and his counterpart on Vancadia."

"Captain Kirk!" Kaulidren had been looking more and more tense from the moment McCoy had returned to the bridge. "Once again I feel it my duty to warn you—these people, these rebel terrorists, cannot be trusted! Bring Delkondros aboard your ship if you must, but don't—"

"Your warning is noted," Kirk said. "Mr. Spock, Dr. McCoy, if either of you has any reservations—"

"Not after that ship was shot down, I don't," McCoy broke in. "Now, are you coming, Spock, or not?"

"I am, Doctor," Spock said, slipping the strap of his tricorder over his shoulder and striding to the turbolift to join McCoy.

As the door hissed shut, Kirk turned toward the communications station. "Lieutenant Uhura, can you get Delkondros again?"

"Yes, sir." Her fingers darted across the panels. "Go ahead, Captain."

"President Delkondros," Kirk said, "two of my men—Lieutenant Commander McCoy, our chief medical officer, and Commander Spock, our science officer—are ready to beam down to the coordinates you gave the transporter room."

"I am most gratified," Delkondros's voice came back. "I am sure that once they have seen our evidence—"

"I'm sure they will evaluate it impartially," Kirk said.

"Of course. That is all we ask."

Kaulidren grimaced but stayed silent.

A minute later the link to the transporter room opened. Kirk suppressed a smile as he heard McCoy's voice in the background, unintelligible but obviously disgruntled, lecturing Spock about something. Abruptly it was cut off.

"Ready, Captain," the transporter chief announced after a couple seconds' hesitation.

"Proceed, Mr. Kyle," Kirk said, sitting back down

in his chair. "But be ready to beam them up at the first sign of trouble. Keep a lock on their communicators."

"Yes, sir." A pause, and then, "Energizing now."

The bridge fell silent, Kirk once again glancing at Kaulidren, trying to fathom the expression on the Premier's bearded face. Fear? Anger?

"They're down, sir," Lieutenant Pritchard at the science station announced, "at the prescribed coordinates."

"Lieutenant Uhura, are you still in contact with Delkondros?"

"No, sir. He ceased transmission when Mr. Spock and Dr. McCoy were being beamed down."

Kirk frowned. "Get him back."

"Yes, sir," Uhura replied, her fingers darting across the controls.

"I warned you, Captain," Kaulidren began, but Kirk cut him off with a gesture, swiveling around to face Pritchard at the science station.

"Lieutenant—"

"Some kind of shield, Captain. It's blocking the sensors."

"Radio transmissions being blocked too, sir," Uhura said, concern evident in her voice.

"Transporter room," Kirk snapped, "bring them back, now!"

Impossible! The thought flashed uselessly through Kirk's mind even as he spoke. *These worlds are at least fifty years away from any type of shield! According to the initial survey—*

"Trying, sir, but we've lost the lock on their communicators and—"

"The shield, yes. Be ready the instant it goes down. Mr. Pritchard, analysis of the shield. Can it be neutralized? Or penetrated?"

"Penetrated, yes, by our weaponry. It appears intended primarily to block electromagnetically based communications in normal space. It would offer some resistance to material objects such as photon torpedoes and to phaser fire, but not enough to block either. Even a low-power phaser burst would be able to—"

"And the transporters?"

"If the power could be stepped up—"

"I wouldna' chance it," Scotty interrupted, crossing the upper deck of the bridge to stand next to Uhura, "except as a last resort. A wee bit o' scramblin' is all it would take."

"Understood, Mr. Scott. Lieutenant Pritchard, you said the sensors were blocked as well. That would mean the shield has a subspace component as well."

"It does, Captain, but the subspace component seems—well, 'accidental,' I suppose you could say. Just a side effect of the shield itself."

"Then it doesn't actually block the sensors?"

"Not completely, sir. It's more like—like static. A lot of detail is lost, and what detail there is, is probably not reliable."

"How much of the planet is affected?"

"Approximately ten thousand square kilometers, sir."

"It's visible on the screen, Captain," Sulu volunteered.

Kirk abruptly turned back to the forward viewscreen. They were passing over the night side of the planet, but that had little effect on the sensors. For the most part, the world looked like any other class-M planet with its oceans and land masses and clouds—except for a single circular area along the jagged coastline of a roughly diamond-shaped continent that filled half the southern hemisphere. There, despite an almost total lack of clouds, the surface looked indistinct, almost fuzzy, and for over a hundred kilometers the line between water and land, sharply delineated at all other points, was not only blurred but appeared to waver, as if seen through a distorting lens that was constantly being shifted.

"Would a world at this technological level have the power necessary to produce a shield like that?" Kirk asked, already knowing the answer.

"I wouldna' think so, Captain," Scott responded. "For a shield o' that size, only antimatter would do the job."

"Which, according to the Federation survey less than ten years ago, would not be technically achievable by either world for another century."

"Aye, Captain, and even with the power, there's the wee matter o' knowing how to generate a shield in the first place. I dinna see how they could manage, at least wi'out outside help."

"My thoughts exactly, Mr. Scott," Kirk said, grimacing as an image of his old friend Tyree, the leader of the hill people on a primitive world, forced its way into his mind. There, too, the natives had appeared to make a sudden technological leap in little more than a decade. There the new technology had consisted of gunpowder and flintlock rifles, not a ten-thousand-square-kilometer energy shield, but the unexpectedness, the unlikelihood of the two advances were comparable.

And there, on Tyree's world, the "advance" had been the work of a small band of Klingons, secretly doling out "inventions," subverting the natives and stirring up war.

"Maximum range sensor scan, Mr. Pritchard," Kirk ordered as he stood up abruptly from the command chair and strode to the science station. "If there's any ship in this solar system capable of warp drive, I want to know about it! Or any other shielded areas, on or off the planet."

"Maximum range scan, yes, sir," Pritchard acknowledged, managing a quick glance over his shoulder at the Captain. Kirk sensed the young officer's nervousness and knew his presence was only adding to it, but that couldn't be helped. Spock and McCoy's lives were on the line down there, and he couldn't afford to waste time or energy on Pritchard's feelings.

After a few minutes Pritchard looked up apologetically. "Sorry, sir, but there's just nothing there. Only a Romulan cloaking device could—"

Kirk shook his head. "I doubt that the Romulans are behind whatever is going on here, Mr. Pritchard.

Unless they've changed radically, they're far more likely to challenge the Federation openly than to use underhanded tactics like this. Keep scanning, Lieutenant. Look for anything out of the ordinary. *Anything.*"

Kirk straightened and turned away from the science station to face Kaulidren. "What do you know of this shield, Premier?"

"What should I know of it? I am no scientist. But I warned you of Delkondros' treachery. I—"

"But not of this shield. Is it new?"

"I did not know of its existence, if that is what you mean. As far as I know, they have never used it before. But I can't say that it surprises me."

"Why not? Have they done this sort of thing before?"

Kaulidren nodded vehemently. "Why else would we need to keep the world under constant surveillance? Their ships, even the small ones no larger than the one I came aboard in, are now capable of not just achieving orbit around Vancadia but of making the trip to Chyrellka—and returning! Their source of power—"

"Captain!" Pritchard interrupted sharply. "Shield strength is decreasing rapidly!"

Whirling back toward the science station, Kirk scanned the main viewscreen. The image of Vancadia was shimmering.

And then the distortion vanished, leaving the planet's surface crystal-clear. In virtually the same instant, the link to the surface was reestablished. Delkondros's voice erupted onto the bridge, the words rushed but ominously clear.

"Any attempt to transport your men will result in their immediate deaths."

Kirk's eyes widened in disbelief. Choking down an impulse to ask the man if he were insane, Kirk signalled Uhura to suppress the transmission from the *Enterprise.*

"Transporter room," Kirk snapped, "lock on to those communicators, but energize only on my order."

"Locked on, sir. Ready for your command."

"Lieutenant Pritchard, maximum resolution sensor scan of area."

"Eleven humanoids in the immediate area of the communicators. Impossible to determine identities at this range. No indication of advanced energy weapons."

"Captain Kirk," Delkondros's voice came again, "I know you heard me. Did you understand me?"

"Transporter room, stand by," Kirk said as he signalled to Uhura to reopen the link.

"I heard you, Delkondros," he went on, "but I hope I didn't understand you correctly. Are you saying my men are now your hostages?"

"Essentially, yes. It is the only way—"

"It is the fastest way," Kirk interrupted sharply, "to prove that Kaulidren has been telling the truth about you! Do *you* understand *that?*"

"In the short term, that may be true, Captain Kirk, but we feel we have no choice, particularly since you have taken Kaulidren aboard your ship. *He* is the madman! You have to believe that!"

"I'd be more inclined to believe you, Delkondros, if you weren't threatening the lives of two of my officers! Release them and we can talk. We can beam *you* aboard if that's what you want. We are ready to listen to whatever you have to say, to look at whatever evidence you have! That's why my men beamed down to your planet, to look at your evidence! So if you really have that evidence, release my men and let them evaluate it!"

"That is precisely what I plan to do!" Delkondros retorted. "But not in that order!"

"Let me speak with them," Kirk said tightly.

"I'm sorry, but that is impossible. But I have no wish to harm them, believe me. Only if you force us—"

"Mad!" Kaulidren broke in. "I warned you, the man is totally mad!"

"Security!" Kirk snapped. "Be ready to escort Kaulidren and his men off the bridge, on my command!"

The two officers flanking the turbolift moved forward.

"I am not mad, Captain, just desperate!" Delkondros shouted. "With *him* on board your ship, how could I be otherwise! His lies—"

Suddenly, a bedlam of other voices erupted from the speakers, all shouting at once, drowning each other out.

"What's happening?" Kirk snapped into the uproar.

But there was no intelligible answer—only continued shouting, and then the sounds of things being knocked over, being broken.

And then, suddenly, the communicator channel was open again, carrying the same sounds, like a muffled echo from another part of the room. For a moment it faded in and out, like an antenna searching for a direction, but then it steadied. And a new sound came through, one not coming through on the other channel —something scraping directly against the communicator, as if it were being dragged across a rough surface.

And then, Spock's voice. It was barely more than a whisper, but the precise diction and total control were unmistakable. "Transporter room," it said, "beam us up—now."

"Do it!" Kirk confirmed instantly as he turned toward the science station. "Lieutenant Pritchard, monitor the operation with the sensors."

"Yes, sir. Transporters energizing—"

Over the jumble of voices coming from Delkondros's headquarters there was the sizzling sound of an energy weapon. For an instant it was louder on the communicator channel than on the other, but then, abruptly, the communicator went dead.

"Laser fire!" Pritchard snapped, and then gasped. "Both men—both lifeform readings are gone! They must've been hit!"

"Transporter, beam them directly to sickbay!

Sickbay, incoming wounded, McCoy and Spock, injuries unknown!"

"Lost the lock, Captain!" the transporter chief broke in.

"The communicators," Pritchard said, "they were destroyed by the blast, whatever it was!"

"Transporter, wide field," Kirk snapped. *"Bring them up!"*

"Trying, but something—"

"The shield is back, Captain!" Pritchard announced.

"Increase power to transporters!"

"No good, Captain," the transporter chief's voice responded. "The wide field isn't concentrated enough to allow—"

"Shield strength increasing!" Pritchard said. "The transporters no longer have enough power to punch through, even with communicators to lock onto! Unless the shield can be deactivated—"

"The antimatter the shield needs for its power," Kirk snapped, "can you locate it?"

Pritchard rapidly punched a half-dozen buttons, scanned the readouts. "Negative, Captain. The subspace component of the shield has increased even more than the rest. Sensor readings now appear to be completely unreliable."

"Your scans while the shield was down—did *they* show anything?"

"Negative, Captain. If the power source does make use of antimatter, it must have its own shield."

Kirk slammed his hands down on the arms of the command chair in frustration. "Uhura—"

"All contact was lost when the communicators were destroyed, Captain. I have been unable to reestablish. No response on any subspace or standard frequency."

For a long moment there was only silence as Kirk turned back to the forward viewscreen and the hundred-kilometer circle of wavering distortion that marked the area covered by the shield. It was more pronounced now, with the distortion in some spots so strong it seemed translucent.

His throat was aching, and his stomach felt hollow.

Helpless, he thought, his fingers clenching into fists, *completely helpless despite everything. Shield or no shield, we could have wiped the planet out. But we couldn't save Bones and Spock.*

We can't even bring their bodies back on board . . .

Chapter Four

"DO YOU BELIEVE THAT FRAUD?" McCoy muttered, shaking his head as the turbolift doors hissed shut, blotting out the sight of Kaulidren and his somber retinue clustered on the bridge.

"If you mean, Doctor, did I believe Premier Kaulidren's statements to be completely truthful, no I did not. At this point, however, we have no practical way of conclusively establishing their worth."

McCoy snorted. "So?"

"I am merely suggesting, Doctor, that it would be illogical to totally disregard them."

"For you, maybe. Me, I'd be more worried about beaming down to *his* planet, especially if he were going with us. The Premier scares me a lot more than those so-called terrorists of his."

"I cannot disagree, Doctor. Premier Kaulidren's objectivity does appear to be seriously impaired by a tendency toward emotionalism. Nonetheless, his warnings cannot be entirely discounted. As you yourself have often claimed, the presence of emotion does not necessarily invalidate the—"

"If you're that worried, Spock, you don't have to come along! I can still beam down by myself!"

"I am not 'worried,' Doctor. I am, as I stated before, simply not dismissing Kaulidren's statements out of hand, and I would advise you to retain a similarly open mind on the subject."

"Anything to satisfy your 'open-minded' Vulcan logic," McCoy muttered as the doors opened, and they stepped out into the corridor leading to the transporter room. "But he's just trying to stir things up. Surely you could see that, Spock. And we *both* saw what his 'surveillance ships' did to that ship that was trying to get through to us! Even if Delkondros did send it up just to prove that Kaulidren's bunch would fire on it—well, they *did* fire on it, and Delkondros was right. Whoever shot it down couldn't have known whether there were people on board, not without sensors. That should be concrete enough for your logic to get a grip on."

"Of course, Doctor," Spock agreed as they entered the transporter room, "but the Premier's evidence regarding the colonists' actions was—"

"Evidence we had to take his word for! Even you said there was no way of telling who the people were in those scenes. Who's to say those atrocities he was trying to show us weren't things *his* bunch had done to the *colonists,* not the other way around?"

"Nothing, Doctor. However, when two possibilities

exist, logic dictates that one be prepared for the consequences of either being proven true."

"Logic be damned, Spock!" McCoy stopped at the base of the transporter platform to scowl up at the Vulcan, already on one of the circles. "All it takes is a little old-fashioned horse sense to see through Kaulidren. In case you hadn't noticed, he has a pretty warped idea of how the Federation works! He thinks we're the same kind of bully he is, and he wants us to do the same thing to the colonists that he claims the colonists have been doing to him, only in spades. He certainly wouldn't let a little thing like the truth stand in the way of getting what he wants!"

"I do not disagree with the substance of anything you have said, Doctor," Spock said patiently.

"You sure have a funny way of agreeing with people, Spock! If—"

He broke off as he heard the sound of someone clearing his throat behind him. It was Kyle, the transporter chief.

"Ready, gentlemen?"

With a last scowl at Spock, McCoy stepped up, turned, and centered himself on the circle next to Spock's, then nodded at Kyle.

"Ready, Captain," the transporter chief reported.

"Proceed, Mr. Kyle," Kirk's voice came back. "But be ready to beam them up at the first sign of trouble. Keep a lock on their communicators."

"Yes, sir," Kyle replied. "Energizing now."

McCoy glanced at Spock, shaking his head and

sighing as he saw that the Vulcan was looking downward, his eyes directed inconspicuously at his tricorder, ready to scan its readout the instant they materialized on the planet below.

"Just a logical precaution, Spock?" he asked, but the words were barely out, when the familiar tingle of the transporter field snatched his attention and focussed it on himself.

Truth be known, he thought with a controlled shiver, *being squirted through space by that blasted machine worries me more than the possibility of danger from the colonists, or even from Kaulidren.* It was the one thing he could agree with the Premier about. He would never get used to the transporter, no matter how many times he went through it. Just the idea that even for a few seconds he didn't exist, except as a pattern of energy, had always given him a—helpless feeling. And helplessness was one feeling he thoroughly disliked, particularly when it involved a machine.

He was just starting to grit his teeth, when the transporter energies solidified their grip on him and the room faded from view.

When they released him and he was able to move again, his jaw muscles relaxed and he released his breath in an inaudible sigh of relief. He stood next to Spock on a bare concrete floor near one end of what appeared to be a large, makeshift conference room, two battered metal tables butted against each other to make one long table. The chairs, no two alike, looked like discards from waiting rooms and assembly lines.

Roughly a dozen men stood beyond the table at the far left side of the room, as if to keep as much distance as possible between themselves and the area in which Spock and McCoy had materialized. Behind the men, in a plain, concrete block wall, was a massive metal fire door, its hinges the only part not spotted with rust. In the wall a dozen yards directly in front of McCoy and Spock was a half-open sliding metal door, while behind them, half as distant, was a fully closed wooden door, its paint peeling.

For a moment there was only silence. Out of the corner of his eye McCoy saw Spock look up abruptly from his tricorder and dart glances toward all of the doors.

"I am Delkondros," the tallest and obviously most muscular of the men said as he began to lead them around the far end of the table toward the new arrivals. A full beard concealed the lower half of his face, and bushy eyebrows shadowed his eyes, but his scalp was bare. All the men wore dark, nondescript tunics and trousers, but Delkondros and one other, almost as powerful-looking as Delkondros, also had what looked like old-fashioned projectile sidearms fastened at their waists. "These men are all members of the Independence Council."

McCoy started forward to greet the man, but Spock's hand darted out to restrain him.

"The formalities of our meeting must be delayed for a moment, President Delkondros," Spock said, ignoring McCoy's scowl. "We were instructed to remain in constant contact with the *Enterprise.*"

"You could at least wait until—" McCoy began, but Spock cut him off with uncharacteristic brusqueness.

"I would suggest you not question our orders, Doctor," Spock said, his communicator already in his hand. "As you may recall from our misadventures on Neural, the Captain does not issue orders without good and sufficient reason."

McCoy frowned. "Neural? What the blazes are you talking about, Spock?"

"Spock to *Enterprise,*" the Vulcan spoke into his communicator, ignoring McCoy.

"There will be no response, Commander Spock," Delkondros said with a sigh as he and the others stopped a dozen feet away. "The area is now shielded against all communications." His hand moved to touch his weapon but he didn't draw it. The other armed council member did the same.

Less surreptitiously, Spock glanced down at his tricorder, then looked quickly around the room again.

"Don't do anything foolish, either of you," Delkondros warned.

"What do you think you're doing?" McCoy snapped, scowling at their hands hovering near their weapons. "We're down here to *help* you!"

"We realize that is what your captain said, Dr. McCoy, but—"

"It's also the *truth!*"

"Perhaps it is," Delkondros admitted, "but with Kaulidren aboard your ship to influence him, we do not feel we dare take any chances. Now, place your communicators on the table."

"What for?" McCoy protested. "I thought you said they wouldn't work anyway."

"As long as the shield is active, they will not," Delkondros said, apparently trying to sound apologetic. "But the power required to maintain that shield is more than we can afford for any length of time. Now, please, gentlemen, you are wasting time. Your communicators will be returned when your mission is completed."

McCoy continued to scowl at the President for another second, then shook his head with an irritated sigh. Delkondros' suspicions about the captain were idiotic, but Kaulidren was another kettle of fish altogether. The Premier was obviously the sort who'd try anything. He wouldn't succeed, of course, not with Jim Kirk, probably not with *any* Starfleet captain, but Delkondros had no way of knowing that. And he obviously wasn't about to take anyone's word for it, least of all theirs. No, if he and Spock were going to accomplish anything at all down here, they would simply have to go along with Delkondros' paranoid demands.

"Come on, Spock," he said, laying his own communicator on the table, "let's get this foolishness over with! Maybe then we can get on with what we came down here to do!"

Spock hesitated a moment, then laid his communicator on the table next to McCoy's. The doctor looked up at Delkondros. "Now, what is it you want to show us?"

Before the President could respond, one of the

council members, a small wiry man with hair and beard just beginning to go gray, stepped forward sharply to face Delkondros.

"This is madness!" the man burst out. "I can't let this go on! Surely even *you* can now see you are only making Vancadia's plight worse!"

The President turned a frown on the new speaker. "We've been through this a hundred times, Tylmaurek. I was under the impression you had finally come to agree with my decision."

Tylmaurek shook his head violently. "Can't you *see* what you're doing, Delkondros? You're destroying our only chance! These people want to help us, but if you keep up this insanity, you'll turn them against us! You'll make it so the Federation will *never* listen to us!"

"He's right," McCoy broke in, suddenly heartened by the appearance of someone who seemed to have a little common sense. "Look, I know how you feel about Kaulidren, but kidnapping us isn't going to help, you must know that. It just makes *you* look bad too."

"That's what I *told* them!" Tylmaurek almost shouted as he spun toward Spock and McCoy. "Right from the start, I *told* them they had to trust you. It was the only way. The Federation can't be blackmailed, not by the likes of us!"

He paused, glaring around at the uneasy council members. "Can't you people *see* this? Didn't you hear what they said? And even if they're lying, do you think *this* will make them change their minds? And once we force them to look at our evidence and we release them—how do you plan to control them then? Or do you plan to hold them hostage forever?"

As Tylmaurek spoke, McCoy noticed two council members—a young, beardless man in his twenties and a tall, bulky man in his fifties—were moving away from the group, around the table toward the fire door.

But it was a thin, dark-haired man in the main group who spoke. "Tylmaurek is right," he said nervously, his eyes not meeting Delkondros' eyes. "These people *did* transport down of their own free will. You told us they would never even come near us unless we tricked them. But they did, and now it seems to me we should take them at their word."

"Besides," someone at the back of the group said, "like Tylmaurek says, if they're lying, there's nothing we can do about it. We *have* to take their word for things. We don't have any choice. These aren't just another pair of Chyrellkan bullies."

Delkondros scowled silently for a moment, his eyes darting from face to face. "Does Tylmaurek speak for the rest of you too? Do you all feel this way?"

At first there was only motionless silence, but then, one by one, the council members muttered their agreement. Except for the one member who, like Delkondros, was armed. That one cast a sideways glance at Delkondros but remained silent.

"Very well," Delkondros said finally, "if that is your wish, so be it. Let the results be on your heads, not mine."

"You will lower the shield, then?" Spock said. "And allow us to contact the *Enterprise?*"

"If that is your wish."

"It is."

"Very well." Delkondros nodded resignedly. "I will have the shield lowered." Taking his hand from where it had been hovering near his weapon, he took a communicator-sized device from a pocket and tapped one of the buttons on its face.

"It's about time!" McCoy muttered, starting toward the table and the communicators, but before he had taken more than a single step, the door directly behind him and Spock burst open.

"What the blazes—" he began, but the words were cut off as, without warning, Spock turned and lunged at him, grasping his shoulders and literally diving to the floor with him, leaving him gasping for breath as a pulsed laser beam sizzled through the open door, stabbing a half-dozen times through the space he and Spock had occupied a split second before. One of the pulses caught the armed council member in one shoulder. His weapon, now drawn, dropped from nerveless fingers. Before he could fall, a second pulse hit his chest.

The room erupted into chaos, most of the council members shouting or screaming at once. Some followed Spock's example and threw themselves to the floor, while others turned and raced for the door, and still others remained frozen in shock. Delkondros, snatching his own weapon from its holster, leaped to one side, away from the wounded man. For an instant he pointed his weapon directly at the two *Enterprise* crewmen, but before he could fire, a man staggered through the door, a laser pistol in one hand. Delkondros jerked the muzzle of his own weapon upward and fired at the intruder, the sound thunderous in the enclosed space. The slug—it *was* a projectile weapon—struck the man solidly, sending him sprawling backward, his weapon flying from his hand and through the door behind him, before it clattered to the floor.

Suddenly, there was only silence, and for a moment everyone was motionless, even those who had started to race toward the opposite door. Unlike the others, Delkondros was expressionless, and he was looking not at the man he had just shot, nor even at the wounded council member, but was scowling intently at Spock and McCoy.

McCoy, ignoring the scowl, scrambled to his feet. "Get that blasted shield down!" he snapped, hurrying toward the wounded council member. "We have to beam this man up to sickbay—immediately! Otherwise he doesn't have a chance!"

Kneeling next to the fallen man, he brought the sensor of his medical tricorder to the vicinity of the wounds. "Still breathing," he muttered, "but just barely, and if he goes into shock before we can—"

McCoy broke off, his frown deepening into a puzzled scowl as he moved the sensor back and forth and watched the tricorder readouts. The readings were all wrong, even for a man as seriously wounded as this! The heart rate, even the basic metabolic indications—

Abruptly, he looked up at the President. "Delkondros, who *is* this man?"

"Does it matter, Doctor?" Spock broke in, moving to the table and snatching up the communicators as he spoke, his eyes never leaving Delkondros. "What is important now is to have the shield lowered."

"Darned right it matters, Spock!" McCoy shot back. "Unless my instruments have gone completely haywire, he isn't a man at all! He's a Klingon!"

"Do not be foolish, Doctor," Spock said, again speaking with uncharacteristic force. "He is obviously—"

"That's enough, both of you!" Delkondros said with a heavy sigh. "I should have realized. You already knew, didn't you, Spock? And don't bother to deny it. I saw you checking your tricorder readings from the moment you arrived. And the way you got yourself and Dr. McCoy out of the line of fire, you must have seen it coming."

Suddenly, Spock's earlier actions, his puzzling references to Neural, made sense to McCoy. The Vulcan had been trying to warn him, and he'd been too blasted dense to catch on, and now—

"But it doesn't matter," Delkondros said, shaking his head in mock sadness. "You do know now. You *all* know." His eyes darted briefly toward the other council members. With one hand he tapped another button on the signalling device he still held. With the other he raised his weapon, bringing it toward Spock. McCoy, even as he leaped to his feet, could see Delkondros' finger tightening on the trigger.

But in the same instant, Tylmaurek, less than a meter from the President's side, lashed out and smashed his hand against Delkondros' wrist.

The gun fired, the bullet gouging a crater in the wall behind Spock, missing him by inches as he lunged forward.

Still gripping the gun, Delkondros backhanded Tylmaurek in the chest, the force of the blow lifting the small man from the floor and sending him reeling backward, gasping for breath. Half stunned, he slammed into McCoy, sending them both to the floor in a tangle of arms and legs.

Before Delkondros could level the gun again, Spock grasped his wrist and struggled to keep the muzzle away from his chest. Two more thunderous explosions sent slugs smashing into the floor, scattering deadly fragments of concrete in all directions, but then Delkondros abruptly shifted position and snaked his other arm around Spock's neck from behind, the forearm snapping up against the Vulcan's chin, then pressing crushingly against the tensed muscles of his throat.

Good Lord, he's a Klingon, too, McCoy realized belatedly as he scrambled to get out from under Tylmaurek's limp weight.

As Spock's feet were lifted from the floor, leaving the Vulcan seemingly helpless in Delkondros' iron grip, McCoy managed to get to his own feet and get his medikit open. Finding the hypospray unit, he searched out a vial and snapped it in as he circled behind Delkondros.

Darting forward, McCoy depressed the hypospray against Delkondros' muscular neck, automatically activating it. The hypo gave a telltale hiss, and Delkondros' head jerked around as he tried to turn and face McCoy. But the motion let Spock's feet touch the floor again, giving him back the leverage he had lost, and the two lurched suddenly sideways.

A guttural sound, almost a growl, welled up in the President's throat, and for just an instant, he stiffened, his arm jerking upward, snapping Spock's head sharply backward.

An instant later the arm went limp and fell away. Delkondros' weapon hit the floor, followed a moment later by Delkondros himself as he toppled backwards, landing at McCoy's feet with a dull thud.

"Thank you, Doctor," Spock acknowledged as he turned and raced to the door through which the man with the laser had come.

Slamming and bolting it, he turned back to the crowd of milling council members while McCoy hurried to the man Delkondros had shot. "Is anyone able to shut off the shield Delkondros spoke of?" Spock asked, his raised voice noticeably hoarse from the pressure Delkondros had applied to his throat.

"He's never even told us where the generators are," one of them said, followed by a chorus of affirmations. "We didn't even know a shield *existed* until he hatched this plan of his!"

"Then we had all best leave the vicinity as quickly as possible."

"This man is dead," McCoy said, standing up from his hasty examination of the man by the door, "and human. But I can't leave this other one, even if he *is* a Klingon!"

"We have no choice in the matter, Doctor," Spock said quickly, "if we are to have a chance to survive ourselves. The two who actually fired the laser before propelling this man through the door are also Klingons, and they will be returning. Delkondros himself is a Klingon, and he summoned them. It is a logical assumption that their next course of action will be to kill everyone here, in order to keep their presence on this world a secret."

Taking his communicator, McCoy reluctantly followed Spock as he started toward the door on the opposite side of the room.

"No, this way! Everyone!"

Tylmaurek, though still out of breath from Delkondros' backhanded blow, was back on his feet on the far side of the table, gesturing toward the fire door. One of the two men who had earlier edged away from the other council members was working with the lock.

Glancing at his tricorder, Spock changed direction and hurried toward the indicated door as it came open with a loud scraping sound. "Come, Doctor. We have only a few seconds."

Grimacing, McCoy fastened the communicator to his belt and raced through the door after Spock. "If we get out of this, Spock, maybe someone'll tell me what the blazes is going on!"

When the rest of the council members only continued to mill around, Tylmaurek raised his voice to a near shout. "Everyone, listen to me! Vulcans do not lie! You've all read the information Captain Mendez brought to us about the Federation! If Mr. Spock says Delkondros is an alien, a Klingon, then he is. And if he says that other Klingons are coming to kill us all, then they *are!* If you want to save your lives, follow me, *now!*"

As if to emphasize his words, something thudded against the door Spock had bolted. A moment later the deadly sizzle of a laser galvanized even the most skeptical of the council members into motion. Despite another call from Tylmaurek, however, they all bolted through the door on the far side of the room, one of them pausing long enough to snatch up Delkondros' weapon and throw a look of dark suspicion over his shoulder at Tylmaurek.

"No!" Tylmaurek screamed, but he could only watch them go. Abruptly, angrily, as the last man disappeared into the hall, Tylmaurek turned and followed Spock and McCoy and the other two council members through the fire door. Turning, he grasped the door, struggling to close it.

But it was jammed. The hinges, despite their lack of rust, had let the massive metal door sag until it dragged on the cracked and uneven concrete floor. Spock, seeing the door was caught, jammed his communicator onto his belt and gripped the door and lifted. From the conference room the sounds of the lasers working on the other door grew louder and less muffled. A moment later one of the beams forced its way through and began to burn a jagged furrow in the floor, only inches from the unconscious Delkondros.

As the remains of the door splintered and crashed open, the fire door clanked shut and Tylmaurek rammed home the bolt, sealing the door behind them.

They were in a huge, dimly lit warehouse, crates of all sizes lining the walls and forming shadowy corridors. Tylmaurek immediately started down one of the aisles. "This way," he said, breaking into a trot and waving for them to follow. "We can talk once we're safely out of here. Maybe even make a plan of some sort."

The others took off after him. They continued through the building for perhaps a minute, then Tylmaurek stopped next to a low-lying wooden platform—a loading dock of some sort, McCoy realized. The Vancadian pressed an electronic key against the lockpad of a small door next to the dock, opened it, and stepped through. He darted quick looks up and down the darkened, deserted street, then motioned the others to follow.

"Over there," he said, pointing across the pot-holed street at a densely wooded, park-like area.

As he was locking the door behind them, a faint scream came from somewhere on the far side of the building, then the muffled explosion of a projectile weapon, and the barely audible, but unmistakable, sizzle of lasers. Tylmaurek winced, almost dropping the electronic key as he slipped it into his pocket. When he turned to race after the others, his face was grim.

"What does your machine tell you now?" He scowled at Spock's tricorder as they ran across the street. "Does it know which of my friends was killed?"

Entering the wooded area, Spock paused and looked down at his tricorder, then back up at Tylmaurek and McCoy, who was also watching him grimly.

"I am sorry," he said. "The only lifeforms that register in that area now are Klingon."

Chapter Five

I SHOULD HAVE BEEN WITH THEM, Kirk thought harshly, his eyes still fastened on the ten thousand square kilometers of shimmering distortion that blurred Vancadia's image on the viewscreen.

I shouldn't have given in to those two squabbling egomaniacs! With the three of us down there instead of just the two—

"I *warned* you!" Kaulidren's grating voice penetrated the numbing shell that had sprung up around Kirk's mind. "I *told* you they were not to be trusted! *Now* do you understand what kind of creatures they are? *Now* will you listen to me?"

Kirk, his teeth gritting in sudden anger, spun to face the Premier. "I *have* been listening, Premier, but in all your warnings, I heard nothing about the existence of that shield they put up!"

Kaulidren shook his head sharply, his own anger seeming to match Kirk's. "How could we warn you of something we knew nothing about? We learned of the shield's existence at the same time you did! But surely it is not so powerful—I heard your Lieutenant Pritchard say that it could be easily breached by your weapons."

"Premier Kaulidren . . ." Kirk drew a deep, calming breath. When he spoke again, his voice was calmer, his tone more controlled. "We are *not* here to take sides. And *certainly* not to kill thousands of innocent people, which is precisely what firing our weapons blindly through that shield would do!"

"But now that your own men have been murdered, are you telling me, Captain, that this so-called Prime Directive your Federation makes so much of does not allow you even to *defend* yourself?"

"Of course not! But firing a photon torpedo at a helpless city is hardly what I'd call *defense!* That would be the same kind of genocidal revenge the Klingons engage in!"

"Is it revenge to exact justice when your own men are killed, Captain?" Kaulidren asked. "I tell you now that force is the only language Delkondros and his kind understand."

"Then we'll have to teach them another," Kirk replied simply.

"Captain, Captain . . ." Kaulidren shook his head. "I suppose I should have known better than to hope for decisive, straightforward action—not that I can entirely blame you. I have read the historical accounts the *El Dorado* provided us and seen examples of how your superiors treat anyone who displays a little steel in his spine, a little initiative! Geiken, Wenzler, Carmody . . ."

Kirk blinked, startled by the Premier's words. If the names he had thrown out were truly his idea of heroes, particularly Jason Carmody, then the chances for a peaceful resolution between Chyrellka and Vancadia were remote, indeed.

Carmody, Kirk remembered with a mental grimace, had been in command of the *Chafee,* a small explorer scout in the days before the establishment of the Neutral Zone. Ignoring his subordinates' urgings of caution, he beamed down to the surface of Delar Seven—a primitive world only parsecs from an area of known Klingon activity—in a hurry to check out what proved later to be false readings indicating the presence of dilithium. He and his crew found themselves in the middle of a pitched battle between Klingon-sponsored forces and another native faction, and instead of beaming out immediately, as the Prime Directive—and just plain common sense—demanded, Carmody, when one of his party was wounded, took out his phaser and began firing. He killed or wounded dozens before his men could overpower him and get the entire party beamed back to their ship. The entire crew of the *Chafee* had later gone missing in space.

"I'm sorry you feel that way, Premier Kaulidren," Kirk said, "but it doesn't alter the facts."

"Facts? The facts are that Delkondros has just murdered two of your men, and you propose to do nothing about it!"

"No, Premier," Kirk snapped harshly, "the *fact* is that we don't *know* who killed them!"

"But you heard Delkondros! He *told* you he was holding them hostage! He even threatened to do exactly what he did—kill them the moment you tried to transport them out of there! Surely you—"

"All of that may be true," Kirk cut him off, "but it sounded to me as if a fight of some kind was going on when the killings occurred. What if some other group —some of your own people, even—attacked Delkondros? My men could have simply been caught in the crossfire. Or, for that matter," Kirk added, scowling directly at Kaulidren as a new possibility flashed into his mind, "we have no way of knowing that it *was* Delkondros who took my men captive. For all I know, it could have been one of your own colonial officials *saying* he was Delkondros! This whole affair *could* be nothing more than a bloodthirsty charade, designed to trick us into siding openly with you, even getting us to retaliate against the colonists."

"You certainly can't *believe* something as outlandish as that, Captain!"

If your heroes are people like Carmody, I could, Kirk thought, but he shook his head reluctantly. "Not at the moment, although the more you urge us to retaliate, the more plausible the idea becomes. So please try to understand, Premier. No matter what you may have thought when you requested our help, the Federation does *not* take sides in non-Federation disputes, not under any circumstances. We are not judge and jury, tempting as the prospect might be in the present circumstances. We are, here and now, mediators, and that is all we are, all we *can be!*"

Abruptly, Kirk turned toward the science station. "Mr. Pritchard, set up a program to monitor that shield constantly, something that will alert both the bridge and the transporter room—and engineering— the moment there's the slightest sign of weakening, the slightest sign of any change at all."

"Aye-aye, Captain."

"And as soon as you have that running, get back on that sensor scan. I want to know every ship and every power source in the Chyrellkan system."

"Right away, sir."

"Lieutenant Uhura, open a channel to Starfleet. This has to be reported, not only the deaths but the existence of the shield and all it implies."

Acknowledging the order in a subdued voice, Uhura worked the controls while Kirk settled back in the command chair, bracing himself for what was to come.

Spock's announcement that only Klingons were alive in the area where there should have been more than a half-dozen council members brought a stunned silence from Tylmaurek and the others, then an angry grimace from Tylmaurek. Abruptly, he turned and started into the heavily wooded park at a fast jog. The others followed without objection.

As they ran, McCoy took his communicator from his belt. The presence of Klingons made it all the more imperative that they reach the *Enterprise,* even if they themselves couldn't make it back. Klingons certainly explained why the situation between

Chyrellka and Vancadia had gone to the devil in less than ten years, but it didn't explain why they were here or what they hoped to accomplish. But whatever it was, unless he or Spock could get word back to the *Enterprise* and the Federation, chances were good that they'd succeed. And having the Klingons succeed at *anything* was bad news. The last time they'd gone to the trouble of passing one of themselves off as human, it had been in order to poison a shipload of quadrotriticale on its way to a starving planet they had designs on. No one knew how many would have died if they'd succeeded in *that* little scheme, McCoy thought angrily.

"McCoy to *Enterprise,*" the doctor shouted, flipping his communicator open as he ran. "McCoy to *Enterprise*—come in, *Enterprise!*"

Spock, a few paces ahead, turned his head briefly, then called back, "Doctor, the shield is obviously still up—and just as obviously, it covers a far bigger area than just the building we were in. I suggest we concentrate our efforts on escaping, rather than—"

McCoy shut his communicator in disgust and shoved it back in his belt, almost dropping it in the process. "Dammit, Spock, I *am* trying to escape! I'm a doctor, not a long-distance runner!"

They were still deep inside the wooded area, with no lights ahead or behind. And he was running out of breath.

"Where are we going?" he called out. "And how much farther is it?"

"Another hundred yards or so," Tylmaurek called

back, sounding almost as out of breath as McCoy, "and we'll be out of here, back to where we left our vehicles." There was a bitter laugh between breaths. "We started taking precautions so we'd have an escape route in case the Chyrellkans found out where we were meeting and raided us, but when Delkondros—or whatever his Klingon name is—hatched this hostage plot, and I couldn't talk him out of it, the three of us—" He glanced around at the other two fleeing council members. "The three of us, we hatched our own little plot. These two were going to try to distract Delkondros while I slipped you out. I thought that once we were out of the building, we would be out from under the shield and you could contact your ship, but from what I've heard, I gather I was wrong about that too."

"Looks like it," McCoy managed as Tylmaurek lapsed back into heavy-breathing silence. A few seconds later he brought them to a stop just short of a line of evergreen-like bushes. Beyond was what could have been, except for the softly rounded contours of the houses and the lack of curbs, a somewhat run-down residential street from twenty-first-century Earth. Even the streetlights, circular glowing tubes, were not all that different. There were, however, no people out for evening strolls, though the weather, clear and dry, was inviting. A single vehicle, a dark gray, almost silent hovercraft, hissed by, and when it was gone, Tylmaurek gestured them forward through an opening in the line of bushes.

"The Chyrellkan curfew isn't for another hour,"

Tylmaurek said, beginning to get his breath back, "but no need to take chances."

"But what are we going to *do?*" the younger of the other two surviving council members finally asked, almost plaintively. "Delkondros and the Chyrellkans I can deal with, but these aliens—"

"There is a house," Tylmaurek said, giving them an address. "It's another precaution I was taking, like the escape route. No one else knows about it, not Delkondros or any of the other council members, so it should be safe—unless the aliens have machines like these tricorders," he added, glancing questioningly at Spock.

"I have no way of being positive, Councilman, but I do not believe they would have anything comparable. Even if they did, they would almost certainly not be able to use them to locate and identify specific individuals."

"That's a relief," Tylmaurek said. "From the way you and Delkondros were talking back there, I was beginning to think they were pure magic, and we have enough trouble without worrying about that. For one thing, Delkondros knows the names we've been using since we were forced underground, even knows where we've been living." He paused, grimacing. "I should have killed him, I can see that now, but it's too late. Dr. McCoy, how long before he wakes up from whatever you did to him?"

"I never used that on a Klingon before, so it's hard to tell. He could be awake already, or it could be another hour."

"Then we'd better hurry. We will be safest at that house until we can decide what to do, make some kind of plans. However," he went on to the other two council members, "the two of you have families to be concerned about." He paused and turned again to the two from the *Enterprise.*

"You know more about these Klingons than I do. I read about them in the Federation histories you've given us, but that's all. What *will* they do? Will they try to track us down?"

"What they will do depends on their numbers and their resources," Spock said, "as well as on their reasons for being here. Once they realize you have escaped, however, I would not discount the possibility that they would indeed go to your homes and wait for you to return. Nor would it be at all out of character for them to take your families hostage in an attempt to force you to give yourselves up."

"And if you did give yourself up," McCoy added darkly, "they'd most likely kill you *and* your families. I wouldn't put anything past them. Life, even Klingon life, doesn't mean much to them, unless it's their own. Winning, that's all that matters to them. And to a Klingon, the winner is the one who's still alive at the end."

The two men paled. "They would *do* such things? Threaten our families?" the younger man gasped.

"It is entirely possible," Spock said.

More than just possible, McCoy thought, suddenly realizing that Klingons were even more alien to these people than to himself or Spock. The history of

Chyrellka wasn't filled with the kind of villains, the Hitlers and the Genghis Khans, that would prepare them for the Klingons. They had been at peace for at least two centuries, so even for these men, who had just seen several of their friends killed, it was hard to believe just how far the Klingons would go, that they would go after totally innocent bystanders if it suited their purpose.

"If I were you," McCoy said, his voice soft but intense, "I'd get home as quickly as possible and get your families to that safe house of Tylmaurek's—before Delkondros wakes up and tells his assassination squad where you live."

"He's right," Tylmaurek said when the two still hesitated, turning their shocked, questioning faces toward him. "Go while you still have the chance."

Abruptly, the two men turned and raced down the street in opposite directions.

"Let's go," Tylmaurek said, starting across the street. "My own vehicle is just around the corner." He shivered. "The sooner I get out of sight, the better I'll feel."

As Spock and McCoy followed Tylmaurek along the sidewalkless street, the whine of a hovercraft starting up came from a block behind them, then the hiss as it moved away. A moment later the same sounds came from the other direction. Then Tylmaurek was punching the combination on the keypad lock of a dark green hovercraft and motioning them inside.

He was silent as the vehicle, which was even quieter inside than out, lifted on its cushion of air and darted off down the street. After several seconds Tylmaurek glanced toward them, and McCoy could see the pain and confusion in the man's eyes. "I guess I have to accept the fact that Klingons are here," he said, shaking his head, "but *why?* What are they *doing* here?"

"Causing trouble, obviously!" McCoy snapped.

"But what could they possibly want from *us?* We're nowhere near their technological level, so they can't be after our knowledge. And if they wanted to steal our raw material— We don't even have outposts in three quarters of the land on Vancadia. They could land almost anywhere out there, and we'd never even know they existed, let alone be able to figure out a way to stop them." He shook his head again. "To go to this much trouble, they have to have a *reason.* Don't they?"

"You'd think so," McCoy said with a grimace, "but I wouldn't bet my life on it. At least, not any reason any of us would recognize. I've said it before, and I'll say it again, Klingons do things for no more reason than sheer Klingon cussedness. Hell, I've always thought that was the only reason that other bunch had for stirring up trouble on Neural. After all, what did they *really* get out of it? Even if they'd been left alone, what would they have gotten out of it—besides the pleasure of watching a couple of once-peaceful tribes slaughter each other!"

"It is difficult to say, Doctor," Spock said when McCoy subsided into a gloomy silence. "However, whatever their purpose on Neural may have been, it would appear at first glance that their pattern of behavior here in the Chyrellkan system is generally similar." Briefly, Spock went on to explain for Tylmaurek's benefit how the Klingons had given advanced weapons to one tribe and then encouraged it to make war on another.

"The shield," McCoy muttered when Spock paused, "the Klingons gave them the shield."

"Precisely, Doctor. Tylmaurek, what do you know of this shield? Did Delkondros claim to have invented it?"

Tylmaurek glanced over his shoulder at the Vulcan, then shook his head. "He never said specifically. He didn't tell anyone about it—didn't tell me, at least—until he came up with this harebrained scheme of his. And he said virtually nothing about it even then, except that it would be ready to operate 'when it was needed.'"

"He gave you no specific information at all, Councilman? Not its size? Its range? Who was constructing the generator? How much power it required? Nothing at all?"

"Not a thing. But since I told him what I thought of his plan and started trying to do something to counteract it, we haven't confided in each other all that much. I didn't tell him about the precautions I was taking, and he didn't tell me much of anything except how his plan was supposed to work."

"What about what he said when he took our communicators?" McCoy asked. "About how the shield took more power than you could afford, so it would have to be shut down before long?"

"I know nothing about that, either."

"Looks like he was lying, in any event," McCoy commented, "which shouldn't be that surprising."

During McCoy's last question and answer, Spock had taken out his communicator and tried again to raise the *Enterprise*. Once again he failed, but this time, instead of returning the device to his belt, he turned it over, removed the back, and studied it briefly. Finally, he closed it and returned it to his belt and transferred his attention to his tricorder.

"If I am not mistaken, Councilman," the Vulcan said after a moment of studying the readouts, "the source of power for this city is nuclear fusion. The generating plant is located approximately fifteen kilometers due north, is that correct?"

Tylmaurek frowned but didn't take his eyes from the street. "That's right. How did you know?"

"It registers quite clearly on the tricorder," Spock explained. "What is puzzling is the fact that I can find no indication of the existence of an energy shield of any kind."

A sudden burst of hope surged through McCoy. "Maybe they finally shut it down!" he muttered as he snatched his communicator from his belt and snapped it open. "Or it blew a fuse. McCoy to *Enterprise*. McCoy to *Enterprise*. Come in."

But there was no answer.

The momentary elation was gone as quickly as it

had come. "Maybe my communicator is damaged," he said, still not ready to give up entirely. "Spock, what about—"

"No, Doctor, according to the tricorder, it is functioning precisely as it was designed to do. The problem is obviously elsewhere, perhaps even on the *Enterprise.*"

"The *Enterprise?* What could be wrong there?"

"Since I am not there, I could not say."

Suddenly McCoy's mind was racing. "If the Klingons are involved—look, Spock, what if the Klingons have come up with some new type of shield, something that doesn't show up on the tricorder?"

"That, too, is of course a possibility. It does not, however, suggest a solution to our current problem."

"It would at least mean that the problem was down here, not on the *Enterprise.* And we could try driving like the devil away from here. Maybe we could get out of the shield's range."

"Which would have to wait until tomorrow in any case," Tylmaurek said, "unless you want to be stopped for curfew violation."

Spock's reply was cut off by a beeping sound and a small flashing light on the control panel of the hovercraft. Tylmaurek frowned and reached for a switch next to the light.

"What *now?*" he muttered and then went on to explain. "That means the government—the Chyrellkan colonial government—has taken over all broadcasts, and they have a message for us."

By the time Tylmaurek had finished speaking, a pair

of tiny screens—one in the front next to the still-blinking light, one embedded in the back of the front seat—lit up.

"Must be really urgent," Tylmaurek said, frowning. "They usually don't put video on signals going to vehicles in motion."

A sharp-faced man in a dark uniform with small patches of the green-and-red Chyrellkan colors on the sleeves appeared.

"The planetary governor," Tylmaurek said disgustedly. "His name is Ulmar."

"Citizens of Vancadia," the governor began, bringing an even more pained expression to Tylmaurek's face, "I come to you today with information that could mean life or death for both of our worlds. However, because I am not unaware of the ill feeling that many of you harbor toward the Chyrellkan colonial administration, I will not deliver this information myself. There must be no possibility that the message will be dismissed because of your mistrust of the messenger. It is too vital for that. Therefore, I will allow the man who brought the information to my attention to present it."

The governor paused, glancing to one side, and for the first time his facade of official calmness slipped, letting a flash of jangling nervousness show in his eyes and in a momentary twitch of his lips.

Then he was facing the camera again. "Citizens of Vancadia, the President of the Vancadian Independence Council."

The screen flared into blankness for a moment, then

steadied as the governor's face was replaced by that of Delkondros.

"I urge every one of you to listen to me, to believe me," Delkondros' image on the tiny hovercraft screens began without preamble. "I have given up my freedom to bring this message to you. It is that important. To get Governor Ulmar to listen to me, to get him to allow me to make this broadcast, I had to give myself up. What I have to say is that important, that vital!"

He paused, swallowing in a fair approximation of a nervous human. "As you all know," he resumed, "the Chyrellkans some time ago requested the help of the Federation in resolving the disputes that have recently developed between our worlds. At one time, I had hoped that once here, the Federation representatives might actually listen not only to the Chyrellkans who had summoned them, but to us. Now, however, it has become obvious that that hope was impossibly naive, even more naive than many of your own hopes that Chyrellka would one day treat Vancadia fairly. But we are not the only victims of that naiveté."

He paused again, as if to get his thoughts back on track from his brief digression. "The Federation's help has arrived. A Federation vessel took up orbit around Chyrellka only hours ago. We have no way of knowing what it is doing there. All communications with Chyrellka were cut off within minutes of its arrival, and neither I nor the governor has been able to reestablish contact. We do, however, know that a

Federation vessel is now orbiting Vancadia. It may be the same vessel, or it may be a second one. But that is not important. What is important is that we *do* know what the personnel of *that* vessel have done. We have seen the kind of 'help' the Federation has sent us."

Abruptly, Delkondros' face vanished, replaced by a view of the room Spock and McCoy had escaped from. The body of the other Klingon council member lay where it had fallen, but the body of the man who had been thrust into the room with the laser pistol in his hand was gone.

But that was only the beginning. Seven more council members lay scattered about the floor, along with three other men that neither Spock nor McCoy recognized. All were obviously victims of laser fire.

"How did *they* get there?" Tylmaurek almost gasped.

"Who are they?" Spock asked as the camera lingered on the bodies.

"Chyrellkans," Tylmaurek said disbelievingly. "Chyrellkan colonial supervisors, two of them from the governor's personal staff!"

"*This* is the 'help' the Federation has given Vancadia," Delkondros resumed. "I am sure you will recognize members of both the Independence Council and the governor's staff. A meeting was being held, on neutral ground, between some of our council members and people from the governor's staff, people with whom we have been keeping in secret contact since we were declared criminals. It was the first meeting, however, the first real truce between us in more than a year, and it was held because of the arrival of the Federation vessel. We hoped, all of us—"

Delkondros broke off, shaking his head in another good approximation of how a human behaves under stress. "I can't remember what we hoped for," he said, his voice suddenly intense, "but what the Federation *sent* was an assassination team responsible for the slaughter you have just seen! These men, mark their faces well!"

For another instant Delkondros' face remained on the screen, but then it was replaced by a pair of obviously computer-generated images, side by side. Presumably based on Delkondros' memory, they were not quite perfect in a dozen tiny ways. Coloring was just a shade off. Shapes of noses, chins and ears were subtly distorted, their expressions coldly menacing.

But there was no mistaking the faces of Spock and McCoy.

Chapter Six

"PERHAPS ANOTHER SHIP should take over the mission, Jim." Admiral Brady's weathered face filled the screen. "We could have a replacement under way within twenty-four hours."

"No, thank you, Admiral. I prefer to see it through myself."

"I know you do, Jim, but under the circumstances—"

"Under the circumstances, Admiral," Kirk said, his voice tight, "it is my responsibility and no one else's. If you doubt my ability to remain objective, you can order me to leave, but that is the only way I will go."

Brady's image studied Kirk silently for several seconds. Finally he nodded. "There was a time when I might have," he said quietly, "but not anymore. Keep us informed. I will notify Sarek and Amanda. And Commander McCoy's daughter. What is her name, Jim?"

"Joanna. But don't do it yet, Admiral."

"Why not? Do you wish to do it yourself?"

"As a matter of fact, yes, I do." Truth be told, he couldn't bear the thought of anyone else delivering the news. But it wasn't only that. "Admiral . . ."

"What is it, Jim?" Brady asked when Kirk didn't continue. "Is there any doubt that they were killed?"

Kirk swallowed. "Not really, sir, but—"

"I understand. Until you actually see the bodies, there is always room for doubt. Very well. When you are satisfied, you will notify the survivors. In the meantime I will order a review of the records of all contacts with non-Federation worlds for other evidence of external influence, Klingon or otherwise."

"There is other evidence *here,* Admiral," said Kaulidren, unwillingly silent until now. "Now that I have heard you and Captain Kirk speak of these Klingons and their disruptive ways, I can see it."

Kirk turned sharply to the Chyrellkan. "What evidence, Kaulidren? Something other than the shield?"

Kaulidren nodded emphatically. "You were interested in causes of the current state of affairs between our worlds, Captain. Well, I will now tell you one of the chief things that drove us apart—the Vancadians' apparent invention of an improved interplanetary drive."

"But wouldn't a better drive have just the opposite effect?" Kirk asked, frowning. "It should make it easier to travel between the planets, easier to keep in touch."

"If *we* had discovered it," he said, "that is what would have happened. But we didn't. The Vancadians did. Or were given it by these Klingons of yours. In any event, this discovery is what made it necessary for us to place surveillance ships in orbit around Vancadia."

"Explain, Premier," Kirk said with a frown as Kaulidren paused.

"It's quite simple. As I'm sure you know, we use shuttles to get into and out of orbit. All interplanetary flights are made in ships built in Chyrellka's orbital factory. Or they were until four years ago, when someone on Vancadia developed an improved drive of some kind. It enabled them to reach Chyrellka in a single ship, little larger than our own shuttles. And they could make the trip in a matter of hours, not the days that it took—still takes—our own ships."

"And why did this make the surveillance ships necessary?" Brady asked impatiently when Kaulidren paused again.

"Because the Vancadians used their ships to try to destroy our capability to reach Vancadia at all," Kaulidren said angrily. "This was when Delkondros was agitating for instant independence, so I can only assume he decided to make sure they achieved it. If we were physically cut off from Vancadia, he assumed we would have to let them go, so that is precisely what he tried to do. First he attacked and destroyed a fleet of our own interplanetary vessels. Until that happened, we hadn't even known that these improved ships existed. And at almost the same time, a second of his ships attacked our factory satellite. By sheer luck something went wrong with the new drive, and the Vancadian ship destroyed itself before it could do more than minor damage to our factory."

"And since then?" Kirk prompted.

"Since then we have managed to regain control of the situation. We haven't been able, obviously, to rid ourselves of Delkondros, but we have at least driven him and his terrorists underground. But we were lucky. If Delkondros hadn't been overeager to use his first two ships, I don't know what would have happened. But he did use them. He was too impatient to wait ten years for the promised independence, and he was too impatient to wait for the new drive to be perfected. He attacked, and lost his only two fully operational ships. And before he could launch more, we were able to arm several of our own ships and put them in orbit about Vancadia. In effect, we put a lid on him. Even so, he attempted three more launches in the following months—and not just remote-controlled ships like the one today—but we were able to shoot them down before they achieved orbit. And then even he realized he was beaten, and he quit."

"And you're sure the ships you shot down were equipped with the improved drive? And were armed?"

"We couldn't be positive, of course, not without sensors such as yours." Kaulidren glanced toward the science station. "But we couldn't take chances. Surely you can see that. If those ships had been allowed to escape Vancadia's gravity well, their power and maneuverability would have made them exceedingly dangerous. That first one destroyed a half dozen of our own ships before we were able to down it. We obviously can't allow that to happen again."

"And who was responsible for developing this improved drive?" Kirk asked.

Kaulidren shook his head with a scowl. "They, of course, have never told us. Delkondros has even denied its existence, not only to us, but to the Vancadians themselves. He tells them we made it all up so we would have a reason for keeping tighter control on their shuttle flights. And for denying them their independence. We have, however, been able to ferret out some rumors regarding the drive's origin."

"And those rumors . . . ?"

"That one of their scientists, one trained on Chyrellka more than a decade ago, developed the theory behind the improvement. But this so-called inventor was conveniently killed in an early test flight. His notes were said to have survived, and others were able to complete his work. All this, of course, happened long before we put our surveillance ships in orbit, so we have no way of knowing what part, if any, is true."

"This scientist was someone known to you?"

"Not personally, of course. At the moment I don't even remember his name, but I do remember that we checked his academic record at the Chyrellkan university where he studied. He was near the bottom of his class in almost everything. It was definitely not the record you would expect of someone who was going to make a major scientific discovery."

"But he did," Kirk said when Kaulidren fell silent, "and you therefore assume he had help."

"Now that I know that such help may have been available to him, yes. It would appear to be the only reasonable explanation."

"Does a sensor scan of the system show anything, Jim?" Brady broke in from Starfleet Headquarters.

"Nothing, Admiral. Other than the *Enterprise,* there are no ships within sensor range capable of warp drive, nor are there any antimatter power sources."

"And none could be concealed by the shield itself?"

"No, Admiral. The shield would prevent us from precisely locating such things, even from getting reliable technical data about them, but I'm confident it isn't blocking our sensors completely enough to conceal the very existence of an antimatter power generator or a warp drive engine. We are able, for example, to detect a nuclear fusion power generator somewhere under the shield. All we do not know are its precise size and location."

"I see." Brady was silent a moment, then nodded almost imperceptibly. "It is your evaluation, then, that while Klingons may have intervened on these worlds in the recent past, they have since withdrawn?"

"Or are lying low while we're in the vicinity," Kirk acknowledged. "We have no way of knowing if individual Klingons—or other aliens, for that matter—are still present and active."

"But I trust your first priority will be to find out, one way or the other."

"Of course, Admiral."

"Very well, Jim. Carry on. And remember—help is available if you decide it is needed."

"I understand, Admiral. Thank you."

"Keep us informed," Brady said brusquely, and a moment later the screen went blank.

Kirk turned to Kaulidren. "Premier Kaulidren," he said quietly, "if Klingons gave the Vancadians the shield and the improved drive, they may have given them more. They may *be* giving them more even now, including something that would allow them to knock out your so-called surveillance ships from the ground. So I would advise you, Premier, to tell us *everything*, not just the alleged terrorist activities the Vancadians have been engaging in. If there really is Klingon involvement here, what's happened so far could be only the opening act."

"These are the ones responsible for the slaughter you have just seen," Delkondros repeated harshly as Spock's and McCoy's features continued to be displayed on the tiny screens. "They appeared in our midst and began shooting, without warning, without reason. I somehow managed to escape, I still don't know how."

Delkondros paused, as if needing to calm himself and collect his thoughts before going on, but during the silence, three new faces appeared. This time they were photographs, not computer-generated images. Tylmaurek, still at the controls of the hovercraft, gasped as he recognized his own face and those of the other two surviving council members.

"And *these* are their collaborators," Delkondros' voice continued, "the traitors who led them to us! We don't know how long those three have been in communication with the Federation. Nor can we be certain what the Federation promised them for their help, nor even what the Federation hopes to gain by this bloodthirsty behavior. The fact that they have slaughtered half the council—as well as members of the governor's staff—however, suggests very strongly that they plan to murder *all* leaders on both sides and put Federation puppets in their places."

The words stopped. Delkondros' face reappeared on the screen.

"Obviously, their work is not done," he resumed grimly. "I can only assume there are more killings planned, many more, including my own and the governor's. That is why I am telling you this. *These killers are still here!* The Federation's assassination squad and their collaborators are still on Vancadia, very likely here in our capital city, going calmly about their business. They must be stopped!"

Again the five faces appeared. "These are the ones," Delkondros repeated. "Watch for them but do *not* approach them, not under any circumstances, not if you value your life! Contact the authorities, and they will handle them."

Delkondros fell silent, but the faces remained on the screen. After a few seconds their names appeared beneath their faces, and then, in a narrow band across the top of the screen, appeared a condensed version of the warning Delkondros had just given, telling anyone who saw any of these people to notify the governor's office. After another minute the governor reappeared, and the whole process began again, apparently the beginning of an endless loop that would continue until Spock and McCoy and their "collaborators" were captured or, more likely, shot on sight.

"This changes everything," Tylmaurek said weakly. "The house I was taking you to won't be safe, not after that mass of lies. Someone's sure to have seen me there, and they don't have any reason not to believe—"

He shook his head, his expression one of disbelief. "It's like Valdreson said—the Chyrellkans I can deal with, but this—look, Spock, Dr. McCoy, you've dealt with these Klingons before, haven't you? Do *you* have any ideas?"

"If you mean, Councilman," Spock said, "do I have any suggestions as to a specific course of action that would extricate us from our current situation, I do not. You would yourself appear to be in a better position than I to analyze the situation, since a thorough knowledge of the local people is likely to be more useful toward that end than would be a similar knowledge of Klingons. However, I would point out that, based on the story Delkondros concocted and on his strident warnings that the five of us are to be avoided at all costs, it is logical to assume that one of his goals, in addition to capturing or killing us, is to keep us from talking to anyone in the meantime. That, in turn, suggests that he fears we would reveal the truth of the situation and that there is at least a chance we would be believed."

McCoy brightened, then nodded as he turned back to Tylmaurek. "I hadn't thought of it quite like that, but Spock's right. But right now the first order of business is to get out of sight and stay alive until we can figure out a way to either contact the *Enterprise* or talk to someone down here without getting shot full of holes." He glanced around at the street, which was deserted except for an occasional parked vehicle. He had seen only four moving vehicles since they had emerged from the park. "And if we're the only car on the road, staying out of sight won't be easy. Is it like this *everywhere?*"

"Probably," Tylmaurek acknowledged with a shudder. "And if it isn't, it will be in a few minutes. The governor's curfew—it's been in effect for more than a month, ever since his oldest son was killed by a bomb probably meant for him. Very few people even dare to leave their homes after dark. No, we have to get off the streets or we won't *have* to be turned in. The governor's nightly sweeps will get us."

McCoy groaned and gave his communicator one more try. "You'd better find us a bolt hole pretty soon, Councilman," he said as he flipped it shut. "There must be *someone* you can trust."

Tylmaurek shook his head bleakly. "At this point I have no idea whether there is or not. Ten minutes ago I could have named a hundred people, but after that broadcast . . . You could be right about Delkondros

94

being afraid we'll talk to someone, but that doesn't help me figure out who we'd have the best chance approaching."

"As a starting point, Councilman," Spock said, "who in authority do you know who is definitely not a Klingon?"

"How should I know? I didn't even suspect Delkondros, and I've known him for years, ever since he was elected to the Council!"

"There are a number of logical criteria you could apply," Spock went on. "First, is the person someone who has a family that is still living? Does the governor, for example, have more family beyond the son you said was killed?"

"Two other sons and a daughter. And a wife. But does that mean he's definitely not a Klingon?"

"Nothing is one hundred percent certain, Councilman, but it is an indication. Another indication would be the manner in which he was elected."

"He wasn't elected, he was appointed—almost fifteen years ago. But what does the way someone is elected have to do with whether or not he could be a Klingon?"

"Based on what both Delkondros and Kaulidren said to the captain, it is my understanding that Delkondros was first elected to the Council following the murder of his chief opponent."

"But that was done by the Chyrellkans," Tylmaurek objected. "They've been conducting a campaign of—" Tylmaurek broke off, his mouth dropping open. "So *that's* how they did it!" he said harshly. "They put

Delkondros up and killed the only other candidate who had a chance of beating him!"

"Their operations are probably more sophisticated than that," Spock said, "but I suspect that in essence, that is precisely what they did. May I assume there are a number of other similar instances?"

"At least a hundred in the last five years!" Tylmaurek shook his head. "In fact, all those deaths, the poisonings—they were one of the reasons we wanted you to come down here. We had always thought—had always been *told*—that the Chyrellkans were responsible, that it was their way of making sure that people they didn't approve of didn't get elected! But it must have been the Klingons who were doing all the killing! Unless—Could these Klingons have formed an alliance with the Chyrellkans? Could they be working together? Could that whole story about Delkondros giving himself up to the governor be a sham?"

"It is a possibility to be considered," Spock admitted, "particularly in light of the remarkable speed with which Delkondros' supposed surrender was accomplished."

Tylmaurek blinked. "You're right. I would've seen it myself if I—if I'd been thinking instead of going into a panic over the lies he was telling about us. There wouldn't have been time for—" Tylmaurek broke off, his eyes widening. "Could Governor Ulmar himself be a Klingon after all?"

"Anything is possible, Councilman," Spock said,

"but it is more likely, considering other factors, that he, like yourself, has simply been taken in by them."

"What about the *Chyrellkan* government?" McCoy asked abruptly. "What about *Kaulidren?*"

"It is, of course, possible he is a Klingon, Doctor, but highly unlikely. It would be foolhardy for even the most human-appearing Klingon to willingly board the *Enterprise.* It would take only the most rudimentary of sensor scans to reveal his true nature, just as Delkondros' true nature was instantly apparent to a simple tricorder scan."

"What's foolhardy for a Vulcan might make perfect sense to a Klingon, Spock," McCoy retorted. "Any race that considers assassination to be an acceptable —an *admired* method of career advancement is a race that has its bolts snugged down a little too tight for its own good!"

"I cannot disagree with your colorful metaphor, Doctor," Spock said, glancing once again at the deserted streets the hovercraft was speeding through. "However, it does nothing toward finding a solution to our current predicament. Councilman, have you yet been able to think of someone who would trust you enough to give you a hearing?"

"There are several I'm almost certain aren't Klingons, but after that broadcast—" He broke off, shaking his head. "After that broadcast, if I didn't know the truth, *I* wouldn't trust even *me.*"

Chapter Seven

AFTER TWO HOURS in the briefing room with Kaulidren, Kirk was convinced that Klingons were indeed involved in events on Vancadia.

But belief was one thing, proof another. The mere existence of anomalous technological advances, even major ones, did not prove that those advances were the result of off-world interference, let alone the result specifically of Klingon interference. There were such things as home-grown geniuses. And the sudden eruption of hostilities between previously friendly factions *certainly* wasn't evidence of off-world interference. Several millennia of history on Earth and dozens of other class-M planets had proven—a thousand times over—that seemingly intelligent beings were quite capable of getting into fights at all levels, from interpersonal to interplanetary, with no outside help whatsoever.

And even if there were proof—

With a grimace, Kirk remembered the thoroughly

unsatisfactory conclusion to the Neural affair. Regardless of their good intentions, the Federation had, of necessity, descended to the Klingons' level and given the same kinds of weapons to the Hill People as the Klingons had given to their enemies.

Nothing remotely similar could be allowed to happen here, not at these technological levels, no matter how happy it would make Kaulidren to get his hands on something that would match or surpass what the Vancadians had—probably—already been given.

"You don't have to give us the actual weapons," Kaulidren persisted, "only the information. We can do the rest for ourselves."

"Impossible," Kirk said flatly. "The result would be the same, in any event."

"The result would be," Kaulidren said angrily, "we would at least have a chance to survive! If you won't protect us even now—" He paused, shaking his head. "Since these Klingons of yours have given the Vancadians the shield and the improved drive," he went on, "what's to stop them from giving them phasers? Or photon torpedoes?"

"Probably very little," Kirk admitted, "as long as the Vancadians are willing to accept and use such things."

Kaulidren snorted. "And why shouldn't they be? Who in their right mind would turn down power like that if it was offered to them?"

"Someone who didn't *need* it!" Kirk snapped.

"Are you suggesting, Captain, that the current

situation is *our* fault? I would remind you that the first thing the Vancadians did with their improved drive was attack us! For no reason whatsoever!"

"I understand that. However, they must have *thought* they had a reason."

"Of course they did! Instant independence! I told you that virtually the moment I came on board! Delkondros had just been elected to the Council, and this was his way of moving up! To becoming President! These Klingons of yours must have worked through him. He was obviously willing to do virtually anything to win! It would not surprise me the least bit to learn that *he* was responsible for the death of his major opponent in the election, the one he accused *us* of murdering! The one whose death he used in his campaign to stir up sentiment against us!"

Breathing heavily, Kaulidren paused to calm himself before going on. "If your Klingons were lurking about, monitoring our communications and broadcasts, that is all they would need to know. They would know Delkondros was a perfect target for them. All they would have to do is offer him the drive. And once he had his hands on that, all he would have to do—all he *did* do was manufacture some lies about us. He blamed us for a half-dozen riots that he probably started himself. He blamed us for one death after another, most of which were either accidental or his own doing. Then he started rumors about how we had changed our minds and were going to go back on our word about granting their independence on schedule!

And then he produced this improved drive you say the Klingons gave him and said, 'Here! This will get us our independence, not ten years from now or a hundred years from now, but *now!*'"

"Assuming that's what happened, Premier," Kirk said, "it's all the more reason not to give you and your world the same weapons the Vancadians have. We have to *stop* this—this escalation, not light the fuse that makes it explode into an all-out war!"

"After what that madman did to your men, you can still talk like that?"

Kirk swallowed away the ache that momentarily gripped his throat at the reminder. "In the first place," he explained deliberately, "we still don't know what really happened down there. Even without the probability that Klingons are involved, anything is possible. And *with* Klingons—possibly with one or more of them down there right now—whatever happened to my men was, directly or indirectly, the doing of those Klingons. Even granting that Delkondros was ripe to be corrupted by them, or that he was already corrupt and was only made more powerful by the Klingons, what about everyone else? You're surely not saying that all Vancadians—all the Vancadians who would be killed if we gave you the weapons you want—deserve to die?"

"Of course not! But if it comes to a choice between their deaths and our own, I'm certainly not going to choose *ours!* And it will come to that, if Delkondros gets more help, if he gets phasers and photon torpedoes to mount on the ships the Klingons have already given him! With phasers, he could bring down our surveillance ships, the only things that are keeping him in check! With one photon torpedo, he could destroy our orbital manufacturing station! With a few more, he could destroy our world!"

Kirk shook his head sadly. "Neither world has to be destroyed, Premier. Instead of trying to counteract the Klingon weapons with Federation weapons, we have to counteract them with the truth."

"And how do you propose to get that truth to anyone on Vancadia? Their shield is still up, and they have refused to communicate with you since they murdered your men!" Abruptly, Kaulidren stood up from the briefing room table. "Further discussion is obviously pointless, Captain. I therefore insist that I be allowed to return to Chyrellka. I have been out of touch with my government for too long already."

Kirk scowled. "Are you so eager to throw away lives, that you won't make the least effort to save them?"

"I *have* made an effort. *You* have made an effort, an effort that has already cost two lives. Continue to make efforts and lose lives as long as you wish, but do so without me. I demand you return me to my world!"

Kirk's scowl darkened for a moment, but then he sighed. "Very well, Premier. We will continue our mediation as best we can without you. A shuttlecraft will be available to transport you and your advisors whenever you're ready."

"A shuttlecraft? But my own ship—"

"—Is incapable of covering the distance between here and Chyrellka unaided, and I am not prepared at this time to take the *Enterprise* out of orbit around Vancadia in order to transport it. It will be delivered to you later, once the situation here is resolved. Meanwhile, you can collect whatever you will need from your ship."

"Captain! That is unacceptable! I demand—"

"I'm sorry, Premier, but for the time being, the *Enterprise* remains in orbit around Vancadia."

"And how long do you intend to keep up this useless observation, Captain? If you refuse to use your weapons, I fail to see what purpose you hope to serve."

"For the time being, we will continue to try to open communications with Delkondros or anyone else we can reach on Vancadia. And we will hope that either the shield comes down or we find a way to neutralize it so we can do a reliable sensor scan of the planet."

For a long moment Kaulidren stood facing Kirk, his fists clenching. Then, abruptly, he turned and stalked toward the briefing room door, his silent entourage of advisors following. Kirk gestured at the security ensign by the door. "Ensign Carlucci will escort you."

"We can find our way to the hangar deck without your assistance!" Kaulidren snapped.

"As you wish, Premier."

A moment later the door hissed shut behind them.

"Hangar deck security," Kirk said into the intercom.

"Yes, Captain," Lieutenant Shanti's voice came back instantly.

"The Premier and his people are on their way down. They will be collecting whatever they need from their ship and transferring it to a shuttlecraft, which will transport them to Chyrellka. Give them whatever help they need."

"Of course, Captain."

"Assign two of your people to the shuttlecraft, Lieutenant, one to pilot it, one to . . . observe them."

"Yes, sir. Brickston and Spencer."

Kirk nodded to himself in agreement. Brickston had a near-photographic memory, and Spencer would easily outbulk Kaulidren's massive guard, still standing statue-like at the head of the Chyrellkan shuttle's steps. "Keep me informed, Lieutenant. I'm on my way to the bridge."

"Aye-aye, sir."

The turbolift doors had barely hissed open on the bridge, when Lieutenant Pritchard's excited voice announced:

"Captain! The shield is down!"

"Transporter room!" Kirk snapped instantly, but before he had completed the words, Kyle was on the intercom.

"Ready, Captain, but—" A brief pause, then an audible exhalation. "But there's nothing to lock on to."

"Lieutenant Pritchard!" Kirk snapped, hurrying to the command chair. "The sensors—"

"Scanning, sir, but there's nothing at the original beam-down coordinates, no lifeform readings at all. And no communicators anywhere."

Kirk nodded, and sank slowly back into the command chair, his eyes sweeping across the suddenly hostile image of the planet on the viewscreen.

No matter what logic told him, he realized, he had not totally given up hope—until that moment. He had admitted as much when he had asked Admiral Brady to delay notification of survivors. As long as the shield had been up, there had been a possibility, no matter how small, that Spock and Bones were on the other side, undetected, and still alive.

But no more.

"Sir . . ." That was Uhura behind him, and he heard the catch in her voice before he turned and saw the mist in her eyes. "No activity on normal subspace frequencies."

Kirk nodded, struggling to maintain his own composure. This was not the time. Spock would have been offended by any lapse in efficiency due to human emotion, even when that emotion was the result of his own death, and McCoy . . .

"Any indication of a shield generator, Lieutenant Pritchard?" Kirk asked, clearing his throat. His voice sounded strained to his ears.

"Nothing detectable, sir."

"No smaller areas still shielded? Particularly at a point near the center of the shielded area?"

"No, sir, nothing. Not even any residual indications

of massive power usage. And no indications of the presence of antimatter. The only major power sources within the shielded area are a pair of stations receiving broadcast power from orbital solar power satellites and a nuclear fusion plant several kilometers north of the beam-down coordinates, nowhere near the center of the area."

"Could these have generated the power for the shield we've seen?"

"Not for the length of time the shield was in existence, sir."

"Lieutenant, are you telling me that the shield that's been covering ten thousand square kilometers can't have existed, that it was an illusion?"

"I—" Pritchard looked momentarily flustered, then collected himself. He shrugged helplessly. "No, sir. It's just that—that our sensors don't provide an explanation for it."

Don't take it out on the kid, Jim. Kirk could almost hear McCoy chiding him. He managed a wan smile and nodded at Pritchard. "Keep looking anyway." He swiveled again in the command chair. "Lieutenant Uhura, any local broadcasts, communications among the Vancadians themselves?"

"None, sir. I have a continuous monitor out for them, but the entire planet appears to be observing radio silence."

Spock and Bones fell into a hole, Kirk thought, *and now the hole has been pulled in after them.* He toggled a switch on the command chair.

"Lieutenant Shanti, is Kaulidren on the hangar deck yet?"

"Yes, sir. He and his people are boarding the shuttlecraft."

"Stop him. I want to talk to him."

"Yes, sir."

After a brief silence Kaulidren's irritated voice crackled over the intercom. "What is it *now,* Captain? Are we being denied the right to return to our world?"

"The shield is down," Kirk said, ignoring Kaulidren's angry questions, "a shield which, according to our sensor readings, Vancadia should not have been able to produce, with or without Klingon help. Also, the entire planet's broadcast communication system seems to have been shut down. Do you have any explanations? Any speculations?"

"None that we haven't already discussed at interminable length, Captain. If the presence of Klingons can't account for your observations, I have no other ideas. Now—am I to be allowed to return to Chyrellka or not?"

"In a minute, Premier." Kirk silenced the channel to the shuttlebay. "Lieutenant Uhura, get Starfleet again."

"Yes, sir."

"Engineering—Scotty, you heard?"

"The shield that canna' exist? Aye, Captain, I heard."

"Any theories? Any more data on the shield? Its power requirements?"

"At least ten times what their nuclear power station could supply, even for a short period. As ye' said, it canna' exist, but it did."

Kirk squeezed his eyes shut in frustration. "What does that leave us, Scotty? The real power source exists but is hidden by another shield? A more sophisticated shield than even the Klingons possess? A shield which our sensors can't even *detect?*"

Kirk stopped. The thought of erroneous sensor readings reminded him of the unexplained computer malfunction that had produced the spurious intruder alert shortly after Kaulidren and his group had come aboard. According to Spock, it had been the result of mutually contradictory readings from two separate sets of sensors.

"Run a complete check on the sensors, Mr. Scott," he said.

"Sir?" Scotty's voice came back. "Are ye' sure? That'll take close ta an—"

"Do it, Scotty," Kirk snapped. "Make it a priority."

"Aye, Captain. I'll get back to ye'."

"Lieutenant Uhura, do you have Starfleet yet?"

"No, Captain," she said, a puzzled frown in her tone. "No reply on any standard frequency. Should I try the emergency band?"

"Run a check on the equipment first," Kirk said, his uneasiness escalating another notch.

"Already run, Captain. No malfunctions indicated."

"I see." He glanced toward Pritchard at the science

station, then turned back to Uhura. "Very well, Lieutenant, try the emergency band."

"Yes, sir."

"And Lieutenant Pritchard, Spock said he had a special program that could be run, something that had a better chance than the ten percent the standard diagnostic programs would have of pinning down the cause of the apparent computer malfunction. Find it and run it."

"Mr. Spock had already initiated the program before he beamed down, Captain." Pritchard paused, leaning over the readouts. "No conclusive results. It only confirms the original general diagnosis, that the problem originated as a result of a conflict between two sensor readings. There is no indication what those readings were or why they conflicted."

"Are there any other tests that could be run, Lieutenant?"

"No standard ones, sir." Pritchard hesitated, his eyes meeting Kirk's for a moment, then lowering. "I understand Mr. Spock had some ideas for special modifications to his own program that might enhance its ability to diagnose problems such as this, in which some or all of the records of the readings that caused the conflict are erased, but so far as I know, those modifications were never made."

And never will be, now, Kirk couldn't help but think, *unless we get another science officer the equal of Spock.* Not a very likely prospect.

"No Starfleet response to emergency hail, Captain," Uhura reported. "Still trying."

"Try for other ships within range. The admiral said there was at least one less than a day away."

"Yes, Captain." Deftly, her fingers darted across the panels before her. "No response," she said after a moment.

Kirk's frown deepened, the feeling of unease again notching higher. "Keep trying, Lieutenant. And Lieutenant Pritchard—"

"Captain," Uhura interrupted, her voice a mixture of surprise and relief, "Starfleet is hailing *us.*"

"On screen!"

"Yes, sir."

Vancadia vanished from the screen, replaced a moment later by an abstract, chaotic swirl. For several seconds it remained, until finally, it resolved itself into a wavering, fuzzy image of Admiral Brady.

"Enterprise," the image began without preamble, "this is Admiral Brady at Starfleet Headquarters. We know you have been attempting to contact us, but something has been interfering with your subspace signal and apparently with our responses. We are using emergency power to temporarily boost our own signal in the hope that it reaches you. We have not yet been able to determine whether the interference is a natural phenomenon or artificial. However, a preliminary review of the records of our contacts with non-Federation worlds in the Chyrellkan sector *has* revealed other indications of possible external influence. Nothing is conclusive, but based on past experience, the Klingons are the most likely to be involved."

The image wavered and almost broke up. When it firmed again, Brady was still speaking. "—an organized campaign, we have been unable to determine." There was a pause. "If such a campaign exists, however, it would seem probable that the Chyrellkan system is involved. But you're the man on the scene, Jim. You can judge better than I, and your interpretation of the Prime Directive as it applies to possible Klingon interference is at least as valid as mine. What I'm trying to say, Jim, is, we have total confidence in your decisions, no matter what they might have to be. You know that. We won't second-guess you in a matter of this importance, where there's a possibility that the security of the Federation is involved."

The image began to waver again. "The subspace interference appears to be getting even worse. Good luck, Jim."

And it was gone in a colorful burst of static.

"The signal is gone, Captain," Uhura confirmed.

"Try to get it back," Kirk snapped, "and *keep* trying."

"Aye-aye, sir."

Kirk was silent a moment as the static vanished and Vancadia reappeared on the viewscreen. There was still no sign of the shield returning. "Mr. Pritchard," he said, "do another sensor scan for the shield—but outward."

"Outward, sir?"

"*Something* is interfering with signals to and from Starfleet. I want to know if the shield was really shut off—or if it could have been expanded, expanded to enclose the entire planet, and the *Enterprise* as well. I know it may sound impossible," he went on, thinking aloud, "but according to your sensor readings, the shield on the planet's surface was itself impossible. As long as we already have one confirmed impossibility, we might as well check for the existence of a second."

"Aye-aye, Captain."

Briskly, Pritchard entered the necessary commands as he watched the readouts.

"Nothing within sensor range, Captain," he said after a few seconds. "No energy fields of any kind, other than those normally associated with planets and stars."

"And there's nothing unusual about those readings?"

"No, sir, all well within normal ranges."

"Captain Kirk!" Kaulidren's voice rasped from the intercom. "My associates and I are still waiting!"

"I assume you have been listening as well?"

"We have, and what we have heard only makes us more anxious to be allowed to return to Chyrellka before the malfunctions—or sabotage!—extends to your drive system and we are stranded in orbit around Vancadia! That may be where *you* wish to spend the rest of your days, but be assured that *I* do not!"

Not quite gritting his teeth, Kirk reined in his anger. "Very well, Premier," he said tersely. The increasingly unpredictable situation made him reluctant to send any of his people across the system in shuttlecraft. "Board your ship. *We* will return you to orbit about Chyrellka."

Cutting off the intercom to the hangar deck, he turned sharply to the helm. "Take us to Chyrellka, Mr. Sulu, full impulse, and then get us back here."

When the hovercraft finally left the city streets and began to make its way across the equally deserted university campus, Dr. Leonard McCoy began to have some slight hope they would reach the destination Tylmaurek had finally selected.

"Only day classes allowed for the duration of the emergency," Tylmaurek explained nervously as the hovercraft skimmed quietly along the smoothly landscaped grounds among the multi-storied buildings. Except for a single hard-surfaced street that ended at the Vancadian equivalent of the Administration Building, there were no provisions for wheeled surface vehicles, only shrubbery-lined lanes through which hovercraft could pass.

McCoy glanced at Spock as the Vulcan made one last unsuccessful attempt with his communicator. McCoy had tried a half-dozen times himself with equal lack of results. As Tylmaurek guided the vehicle through an entrance to the underground parking area that apparently underlay most of the campus, Spock fell silent and replaced the communicator on his belt.

"Still no luck, Spock?"

"None, Doctor," Spock said, an arched eyebrow the

only indication that he found McCoy's question not so much rhetorical as illogical and unnecessary.

"We had best take the stairs," Tylmaurek said as he settled the hovercraft into the first open slot he came to. "There will be less chance of encountering someone, and it will be easier to hide if we do."

"Just a moment, Councilman," Spock cautioned as Tylmaurek started to open the hovercraft door.

"What is it?"

"Two humanoid lifeforms are approaching from our left," he said, looking up from his tricorder.

Tylmaurek ducked down and peered nervously in the indicated direction. "Probably just some students leaving," he said softly after a moment. "Half of the faculty live in this building, and since the shutdown of formal evening classes, some of the professors have been conducting informal ones in their living quarters. It's the only time many of the working students have free."

In the next aisle over, a hovercraft whined to life and departed, not nearly as quietly as the other vehicles they had heard. After a minute there was only silence.

"Is anyone else coming?" Tylmaurek asked, his voice unsteady. "It's already past curfew, so there shouldn't be, but—"

"No one, Councilman. Nor," Spock added, "can I detect any Klingons within the building."

"After that broadcast," McCoy said with a grimace, "it's not just Klingons we have to worry about. Tylmaurek, are you sure this Professor Rohgan is the *only* person you can trust? There isn't someone else, someone who lives in a slightly less populated area? These uniforms and those ears don't exactly blend into the background."

"I'm sorry," Tylmaurek said, swallowing, "but he still strikes me as our best bet. In a way, I'm in the same position now that he was in five years ago," he went on, and as the councilman talked, McCoy began to wonder uneasily if he was as uncertain as he sounded, if maybe he was talking simply to convince himself that he'd made the right decision.

"He was a member of the Council when it was a legitimately elected body, before we were outlawed," Tylmaurek continued. "When Delkondros decided to try to get us our independence by attacking the Chyrellkan orbital factory, Rohgan and a half-dozen others resigned." He frowned. "They *may* even have told the Chyrellkans about Delkondros' planned attack, I don't know. That might be why it didn't succeed. But the point is, Rohgan saw through Delkondros five years ago and disassociated himself from the Council. I haven't talked to him since the Council was outlawed, but now—"

He paused, shaking his head again. "It's just a feeling, but he's the only person I can think of who might hear me out before shooting me or turning me in. And who might be able to get through to someone in authority with the truth about Delkondros. Assuming there is anyone in authority who isn't a Klingon."

He paused, frowning. "Now that I think about it, I'm surprised Delkondros didn't include Rohgan in his list of collaborators. When the Council was first outlawed, after our ships were destroyed, Delkondros wanted to have him killed, but the rest of us were able to convince him it would be counterproductive at best."

"He does sound like our best bet," McCoy said, trying to sound encouraging when Tylmaurek fell silent. "Now, let's get going before Spock tries to change our minds. Or we get caught."

"Why should I attempt to change your minds, Doctor? I agree that contacting Professor Rohgan does offer us the best odds for survival, under the circumstances."

McCoy widened his eyes. "Based on Tylmaurek's 'feeling,' Spock?"

"Of course not, Doctor. My agreement is based on the logic of the rest of what he said. However, I must point out that in this instance, the best odds are not good odds at all."

"And they're getting worse every second we sit around here discussing them!" Abruptly, McCoy pushed open the door and climbed out.

After another quick check of the tricorder, Spock and Tylmaurek followed, and seconds later the three were entering an enclosed stairwell a dozen yards from the parked hovercraft.

"The hallway is clear," Spock said when they reached the fourth floor, and then they were all standing in the spartan corridor in front of a plain brown door.

"Is Rohgan alone, Mr. Spock?" Tylmaurek asked.

"If you mean, Councilman, is there only a single individual in the room beyond this door," Spock said, looking up from the tricorder, "there is. Whether that individual is the one you call Rohgan, I have no way of knowing. Readings do indicate the individual is not a Klingon, that he weighs approximately ninety kilograms, has a physiological profile that corresponds to an Earth human age of approximately sixty, and is currently extremely agitated."

Tylmaurek blinked, then glanced at the tricorder. "I don't suppose that thing can tell you *why* he's agitated?"

"No, Councilman, but logic would suggest that his emotional state is related to Delkondros' broadcast assertions that his world is, in effect, under attack by the Federation. You yourself are in a similar state."

"If you two are finished discussing your emotional states," McCoy broke in, gesturing at the door.

Tylmaurek nodded and rapped sharply.

The door opened almost immediately, revealing a tall, slender man with white, thinning hair. He wore the same kind of loose-fitting tunic that Tylmaurek wore, but with an outer covering, possibly the Vancadian equivalent of a sweater. His eyes widened as he saw Tylmaurek. A moment later, when he darted a glance to the side and saw Spock and McCoy, he involuntarily jerked backward.

McCoy tensed, ready to run, but then, abruptly, a small smile appeared on the older man's face. "Ah," he said softly, "the Federation assassination squad and one of their traitorous collaborators. Do come in, quickly, before some loyal citizen sees you."

Chapter Eight

"ALL SENSORS CHECK OUT one hundred percent, Captain," Scott's voice came over the intercom from Engineering as Sulu brought the *Enterprise* about, aiming it at Vancadia and reapplying full impulse power.

"Communication equipment likewise, Captain," Uhura said a moment later. "But there has been no further response from Starfleet, either to a standard channel hail or emergency."

Kirk let his breath out in a frustrated sigh. The impossibilities continued to pile up. According to all tests, every system on the *Enterprise* was operating at, or near, peak efficiency, and yet in many ways it was as if the ship had dropped out of the known universe. They couldn't get in touch with Starfleet Headquarters or with any ship in space. The thousands of electromagnetic signals that had earlier been evident on both Chyrellka and Vancadia were silent. Even the sensors picked up only the radiation from power lines and the like—no modulated signals, no radio, no television, nothing.

It was becoming more and more as if a shield had been placed not around Vancadia or around the entire Chyrellkan system, but around the *Enterprise* itself. Except, the sensors *were* detecting the magnetic fields of both planets and of the sun itself and were *not* detecting a shield. Perhaps if he sent a shuttle out and compared the readings of its sensors with those of the *Enterprise* itself—

"Captain! The shield is back up."

Lieutenant Pritchard's voice broke into Kirk's speculations on the impossible, but as his eyes darted to the forward viewscreen, he saw that he had yet another impossibility to throw into the equation. The shield was indeed back, but where before its elusive shimmer had covered a circle roughly a hundred kilometers across, it now covered at least double that area.

And now, instead of a faint, ill-defined shimmer, it glittered with a hard-edged translucence.

McCoy realized he had been holding his breath only when Professor Rohgan hastily closed the door behind the three men and turned to face them, the smile gone, leaving only tension behind.

"I assume, Tylmaurek," Rohgan said, "there is a rational explanation for what I've just heard Delkondros claim."

"Lies, every bit of it!" Tylmaurek blurted.

"Our friends were not killed?" Hope flared in Rohgan's eyes.

For a moment there was total silence. McCoy could see Tylmaurek's jaw tremble at the returning pain as he shook his head. "No," he said, his voice cracking, "the killings were real." Swallowing away the unsteadiness, he went on. "I wasn't a witness, but I'm almost certain they were real. I did see Delkondros kill another man, but not one of the council—"

"You're saying Delkondros is the killer?" Rohgan broke in. "Are you positive? I didn't think even he could be *that* mad!"

Tylmaurek snorted, a sharp, bitter sound. "He did it, or ordered it to be done, but it wasn't madness." He glanced at McCoy and Spock. "At least, not any normal kind of madness."

Then he began to explain. As Tylmaurek spoke, Rohgan's eyes widened at first, then narrowed. From time to time he glanced toward Spock and McCoy, as if he could verify in their faces the truth of what Tylmaurek was saying.

When Tylmaurek finished, Rohgan let his breath out in an explosive sigh. "It is your belief, then, that Delkondros is not the overambitious paranoid I have always assumed, but a murderous alien?"

"I know it sounds insane, Professor," McCoy began when Tylmaurek seemed lost for a reply, "but—"

"On the contrary, Doctor—McCoy, was it? On the contrary, it is the first rational explanation I have heard for Delkondros' behavior these last few years.

And something of a relief to my own conscience. Since I left the Council, I have had ample time to wonder if, had I stayed, I might not have been able to influence him toward a less-disastrous course of action. Based on what you say, however, no one could have done that. His words and actions have all been purposely designed to drive our worlds apart, to cause as much discord as possible. But why? What reason could these aliens have for wanting to disrupt our little worlds?"

McCoy gave a restrained snort. "It's part of their job description. It's what they do."

"Even so—" Rohgan broke off. "But I am wasting valuable time," he said, turning sharply toward Spock, his eyes taking in once again the Vulcan's ears, the faint coppery green tinge to his skin, then lowering to the tricorder, still suspended by its strap from Spock's shoulder. "With this device you can detect these aliens, regardless of their outward appearance? And at a reasonable distance? Is that what I am to understand?"

"These particular aliens, Professor," Spock acknowledged, "but not all."

"Are there yet other types involved?"

"Not to my knowledge, Professor."

Rohgan drew in a deep breath. "Then, assuming everything Tylmaurek has told me is the truth, I may be able to get you in contact with your ship. I may even be able to arrange for you to be taken to the ship itself."

Hope flooded through McCoy, sending his heart racing, but an instant later a wave of suspicion struck him like a physical blow as he realized the man *must* be setting them up one way or another. It was simply too good to be true that the first person Tylmaurek took them to not only didn't try to shoot them or even turn them in but had a way of contacting the *Enterprise.*

"How?" McCoy asked sharply. "We've got Starfleet communicators, and *we* can't get in touch with them."

"It's a long story, and we don't have time," Rohgan said. "Suffice it to say, a group of us have been working on a plan of our own. Now—"

Rohgan broke off, gasping, as a siren-like beeping filled the room. "Another bulletin," he said, his voice trembling from the shock of the sudden sound.

Turning, he activated a screen mounted flush with the wall. As it flared into life, the Chyrellkan flag filled the screen, but after only a few moments it was replaced by the governor's face.

But not his living face. It was obviously a still image, a photograph.

Then a voice began speaking, neither the governor's nor Delkondros' voice.

"The Vancadian colonial office regrets to announce that Governor Ulmar and Council President Delkondros have both been murdered by the Federation assassination team."

With the words, the governor's picture vanished, replaced a split second later by the same images of Spock, McCoy, and Tylmaurek that had been broadcast before.

"Only minutes ago," the voice went on, "using

unknown Federation technology, these three were able to pass undetected through the governor's security, kill both Governor Ulmar and Council President Delkondros, and escape. If anyone sees—"

Rohgan tapped the screen into blank silence. McCoy saw that his face was chalk white and wondered if the man was about to faint. Instead, he turned and darted to the door and jerked it open.

"Come with me, quickly! I'll explain as we go."

"Wait, Professor."

It was Spock. Looking around, McCoy saw that he was once again intent on his tricorder. The Vulcan had been glancing down at it every few seconds since the moment they had entered the room, but now he was continuously studying the readings, moving the instrument slightly as he did.

"Three lifeforms have just entered the building," Spock went on, "on the underground parking level. The readings indicate two are human, but the third is Klingon. And the Klingon is carrying an energy weapon similar to the laser that was used in the earlier attempt on our lives."

McCoy threw an accusing glance at Rohgan. It *was* a setup! "What did you do, Professor," he snapped, "trip an alarm when we first came in?"

"No, Doctor," Spock said, keeping his eyes on the tricorder. "According to Professor Rohgan's physiological reactions, he is as startled as you are, perhaps more. But if we are going to leave, gentlemen, I would suggest we do so now. The new arrivals are about to enter the elevator."

Rohgan, who had frozen at Spock's warning, now lurched into motion, racing down the hall. "We can go down the stairs. My—"

"Only the Klingon and one of the humans are entering the elevator," Spock cautioned. "The second human appears to be returning to the vicinity of their vehicle, which I believe has a clear view of the stairwell door."

Rohgan shuddered to a halt at the stairwell door and leaned against it, shaking his head. "We're trapped, then?"

"Not necessarily," McCoy snapped, remembering how they had gotten away from Kaulidren. He still didn't fully trust Rohgan, but the man was definitely preferable to what was coming up in the elevator. "Spock," he said, hastily digging into his medikit, "I still have a couple loads in my hypospray."

"Understood, Doctor," Spock said, his eyes still focussed on the tricorder. "Professor, I believe we will have the best chance of success if you will stand directly in front of the elevator door, on the far side of the hall. Attract their attention as the door opens."

"What—"

"Councilman, stay back, out of sight," Spock said, gesturing with his free hand. "Doctor, the Klingon is on the left."

Hypospray in hand, McCoy darted to the left side of the elevator and flattened his back against the wall. Spock, shifting his tricorder to his left hand, pressed himself against the wall on the right.

"Second floor," Spock said, quietly counting down, "third, and . . ."

The humming of the elevator stopped. Spock closed and released the tricorder, letting it hang from its shoulder strap. For a moment there was only silence, except for Rohgan's nervous swallow.

The door slid open.

The human looked startled as he saw Rohgan standing barely six feet in front of him. He reached for the projectile weapon on his belt, the same kind Delkondros had used.

The Klingon, who looked just as human as Delkondros had, already had the laser in his hand, hanging loosely at his side. He stiffened, then smiled, and started to bring the weapon up as the two stepped out of the elevator.

His arm outstretched, Spock stepped away from the wall. As the human and the Klingon both started to turn toward the motion registering in the corners of their eyes, Spock's fingers closed on the nerves in the man's neck. Simultaneously, McCoy stabbed out with the hypospray, bringing it into solid contact with the back of the Klingon's neck.

The nerve pinch felled the human instantly, but the Klingon had time to recognize the Vulcan and would have had time to raise the laser the rest of the way and fire, had Spock not reached past the falling human and grasped the Klingon's arm, forcing it down and sending the laser pulse harmlessly into the floor. Before the startled Klingon could bring his strength into play and raise his arm against Spock's restraining hand, the injection, made within inches of the brain, took hold. His face just beginning to register rage, the Klingon fell.

As the Klingon hit the floor, Tylmaurek lunged forward and snatched the laser from his fingers. "If I'd done this to Delkondros—" he began, but Spock gripped his wrist and easily turned the muzzle away from the unconscious Klingon. Tylmaurek struggled for a moment but then went limp, letting the laser dangle from his fingers. Despite his angry words, he looked almost relieved that Spock had stopped him.

"If we are to be returned to the *Enterprise,*" Spock said, "this individual will be valuable evidence." He turned to Rohgan. "Will we have far to go, Professor?"

"Approximately two hundred kilometers," he said, swallowing nervously as he tore his eyes from the fallen Klingon and the laser burn a few inches from his feet. "But I don't see how we can make it now. The curfew, the bulletin showing the three of you—"

"Would we have a better chance if we were to use the vehicle these two came in?"

"Probably, but—"

"Then we will attempt to avail ourselves of it." Spock turned to McCoy. "Doctor, Delkondros apparently awakened rather quickly earlier today. Do you have something that will keep this one unconscious for a longer period?"

McCoy nodded. He had already changed the load in his hypospray. "This wouldn't have worked fast enough," he said as he pressed it to the fallen

Klingon's neck, "but it will keep him out at least ten times as long."

Spock leaned down, picked the Klingon up, easily slung him over one shoulder, and headed back toward the apartment. "Do the same for the human," he said, "and bring him along."

Deftly, McCoy again switched hypospray loads— this time to something more suitable to a human metabolism—triggered it against the man's neck, and watched as Tylmaurek and Rohgan lifted the unconscious man and followed Spock and his Klingon burden into Rohgan's apartment.

Less than two minutes later they were headed back down in the elevator, the Klingon on the floor, Tylmaurek dressed in the human's gray, loose-fitting uniform. Stopping at the ground level, McCoy and Rohgan got out while Spock picked the Klingon up and lowered him into Tylmaurek's outstretched arms. Tylmaurek grunted at the weight as Spock released it and backed quickly out of the elevator to join the others. Before the elevator doors had closed on the straining Tylmaurek, the other three were on their way down the stairwell. At the parking level, Spock opened the door a tiny crack and stood watching and waiting.

Within seconds the sound of the elevator doors grating open announced Tylmaurek's arrival. Careful to keep his face averted from the car where he knew the second man was waiting, Tylmaurek lurched out of the elevator, the unconscious Klingon still cradled in his arms. Barely able to support the weight, he didn't have to pretend his unsteadiness as he staggered out and let his knees buckle as he attempted to lower the Klingon to the floor. With his face still averted, he waved urgently for the one in the car to come help him.

After a tense moment the hovercraft door opened and the second man leaped out and came running. "What the hell—" he began, but at that point he passed the stairwell door, and Spock's hand darted through the suddenly widened crack. The man fell as quickly as had his partner four floors above. McCoy scrambled past Spock and applied another hypospray while the two Vancadians deposited the man in Tylmaurek's vehicle.

"If someone finds him there," Tylmaurek said with a sudden tired grin, "I don't suppose it could get me in any more trouble than I'm already in."

A minute later the Klingon was stowed in his own hovercraft's storage compartment, and Rohgan, forcing himself to be calm, was familiarizing himself with the vehicle's controls. Another minute and he was maneuvering it out of the underground parking area and onto the deserted campus.

"Now that that's safely out of the way," McCoy said as they headed back the way Tylmaurek had brought them in earlier, "would you mind explaining how you're going to get us to the *Enterprise?* The last time I looked, hovercraft couldn't quite make it into orbit."

"They still can't, Doctor," Rohgan said with a nervous smile, "although after what you have told me this evening about your aliens and their machinations, it wouldn't surprise me if they could. No, we have a ship that will, I hope, do the job."

McCoy frowned skeptically in the faint glow from the passing streetlights. "What about Kaulidren and his surveillance ships?"

"Our ship can get past them," Rohgan said. He swallowed audibly, as if in a continuing effort to hold on to his hard-won calmness. "Or so I've been assured. However, it's becoming obvious to me that there are no guarantees. And there are any number of uncertainties, not the least of which is the fact that the very device that allows the ship to elude Kaulidren's guard ships may very well be another 'gift' from these Klingons of yours."

McCoy rolled his eyes and glanced toward Spock, who seemed to be taking the information in with his usual stoic passivity. "That's what I'd call one whale of an uncertainty, Professor."

"Obviously. However, under the circumstances, I don't see that we have any choice but to make the attempt, do you? To the best of my knowledge, it is your only chance to get beyond this shield—if that is indeed what is blocking your communicators—and contact your ship."

"Maybe so," McCoy said, "but you said we have a couple hundred kilometers to go. Why don't you explain the whole thing to us—including just how you, of all people, happen to have access to the one and only ship on Vancadia that has a chance of getting past Kaulidren's surveillance ships."

"Yes, Professor Rohgan," Tylmaurek added, a note of suspicion suddenly apparent in his own voice, "I'd like to hear about it too."

Rohgan blinked, darting a startled glance at Tylmaurek. Either he was genuinely surprised at the suspicion he had suddenly been confronted with, McCoy thought, or he was an excellent actor.

Finally Rohgan nodded. "Very well, gentlemen," he said, "but it's a long story."

After his resignation from the Council, Rohgan had secretly kept in contact with the engineers who had worked on the improved drive, most of whom had agreed with Rohgan and had not wanted to use it to attack the Chyrellkan orbital factory. Within weeks of that fiasco Delkondros had them working from a new set of "notes" supposedly made by the same mysterious deceased genius whose earlier notes had led to the drive. These notes described a form of shield that would allow whatever ship it enclosed to slip past Tylmaurek's guard ships undetected.

And Delkondros, to the engineers' horror, was not only keeping the shield a secret from the remaining members of the Council but was planning to use it to finish the job he had failed at the first time. He had managed to keep a ship hidden from the Chyrellkans when the other three had been destroyed, and he was planning to use that ship, with the shield, to destroy the orbital factory.

Rather than go to the Chyrellkans with this information, as he had done when the first attack was planned, Rohgan and the engineers and several of the former council members who had resigned with him came up with their own plan. The engineers began giving Delkondros fake reports, indicating much slower progress than they were actually making. As far as Delkondros knew, it would be another year or more before the first prototype shield could be built and installed. In reality, it had already been built, installed, and tested.

"Our original plan," Rohgan said, "was for a group of us to take the ship out, past the guard ships, all the way to orbit around Chyrellka. Once there, we would let down the shield, let the Chyrellkans see us. And we would announce our peaceful intentions, to prove to the Chyrellkans once and for all that we did not want war, that we could be trusted."

Rohgan paused, shaking his head. "I know it sounds naive, but to us it was infinitely better than attempting to kill those thousands of Chyrellkans in their orbital factory the way Delkondros wanted to do. And if the Chyrellkans agreed, we hoped they would respond in a like way."

McCoy shook his head. He was inclined to believe the man. "More people should be naive like that," he said, "except maybe when they're dealing with Klingons. But this ship—you say it's ready to go?"

Rohgan nodded. "We were almost ready to launch when we learned your ship was on its way here. That changed our plans. We knew that the Chyrellkans would be filling your ears with lies, so we decided to go ahead with the launch as soon as possible after your actual arrival. We would do basically what we had already planned, except we would tell the Federation what we had planned to tell the Chyrellkans."

"Then Delkondros made his broadcast this evening," McCoy said.

"Precisely," Rohgan agreed. "We had no reason to disbelieve it. So when Delkondros told us what you had done, even showed us the bodies of people we all knew, we could only assume that either the Federation was as evil as these Klingons you speak of or that Kaulidren had convinced it to take Chyrellka's side. And that if we approached your ship, we would simply be destroyed.

"But everyone who was to go on the mission had already gathered at the ship. The launch was to be tonight. So those of us who were remaining behind have been trying to get in touch with those at the ship to stop the launch. But communications have been cut off; we don't know why. Some of us started to the ship earlier this evening in hopes of getting there in time to stop them. That is where the two you saw leaving when you arrived at my building were going, in fact. But now that we know the truth, we can still make the launch. And the three of you can be aboard. The ship will take you beyond the shield, where you can use your communicators to contact your ship and inform it of the situation here."

McCoy grimaced when Rohgan fell silent and the hovercraft continued along the deserted streets. He was finally convinced that Rohgan believed every word he had said and wasn't purposely setting them up, but even so, the chances of his actually getting them out in space where they could contact the *Enterprise* were slim at best. Chances were much better that Delkondros and the rest of the Klingons had known from the start about the little conspiracy between him and the engineers. Which meant that, if he and Spock went with Rohgan to the ship, chances were excellent that they would be delivering themselves right into the enemy's hands.

And yet, no matter how he wracked his brain, he couldn't think of a blasted thing to do that would give them a better chance of ever seeing the *Enterprise* again.

Chapter Nine

KIRK SCOWLED at the viewscreen and the now-almost-opaque shield that spread over more than twenty thousand square kilometers of Vancadia's surface.

"Can physical objects still penetrate it, Lieutenant Pritchard?" Kirk asked.

"I can't be positive, Captain, since it now blocks our sensors almost entirely, but all indications are that they could."

Kirk punched a button on the arm of the command chair. "Mr. Scott," he said when the chief engineer responded, "I'm sending a shuttle down. Pick the most reliable one you've got, then you and Lieutenant Pritchard set up an automated program to take it just below the level of the shield. Let's see if we can't determine the nature of the shield, its source, and a way to either bypass it or shut it down."

"Aye, Captain, I'll meet the lieutenant in the shuttlebay."

"Two minutes, Scotty. The lieutenant is on his way."

Still scowling, Kirk turned back to the main viewscreen. It looked as if the shield's strength had increased in the seconds he had looked away.

Hargemon smiled with infinite satisfaction as he watched the *Enterprise,* helpless on the viewscreen before him. The little relay station, firmly anchored to the starship by its kilometer-long tractor beam, was working perfectly. If he wished, he could set the *Enterprise* on an irreversible slide toward destruction right this minute in any of a hundred ways. Kirk wouldn't be able to stop it. Scott wouldn't be able to stop it. Certainly whoever was now manning the science station wouldn't be able to stop it. Only Spock, if he were still on board, might have had a chance of finding the problem and halting the destruction.

And perhaps not even Spock, he thought with a faint tinge of regret. It was unfortunate the Vulcan would not have the chance to try. He had been tempted to give him that chance, but the commander had overruled him. And for once the commander had been right, he had to admit.

But Hargemon's turn would come soon enough.

A test run, the commander had called this project, and he had been correct there as well, though perhaps not in quite the way he had intended.

Smiling, Hargemon thought of the Klingon battlecruiser that would be darting in to pick them up when he and the commander and the others had completed their business in the Chyrellkan system. It would be a good subject for his own "test run." Its computer would be child's play compared to the one on the *Enterprise.* He could have it doing the computer equivalent of handstands in a matter of weeks. Even that fool Kelgar, whom the commander had saddled him with, would be capable of tricking that primitive collection of microcircuits, now that he'd been watching—and presumably learning from—Hargemon.

His attention snapped back to the viewscreen. The *Enterprise* shuttlebay was opening! What the devil did Kirk think he could accomplish by sending a shuttlecraft out?

For a moment a sinking feeling gripped his stomach. Had *Kirk* realized the truth? Hadn't getting Spock out of the way been enough?

But no, it didn't matter. Even if Kirk did realize in general what the problem was, even if he was sending a shuttlecraft out to check his theory, he would never be able to figure out the specifics. Only Spock, who sometimes seemed to live in virtual symbiosis with the computer, could do that—at least, in the time the *Enterprise* had left.

Even so, there was no point in taking even that much of a chance.

His fingers playing over the keyboard he himself had designed, Hargemon entered a series of commands and watched as one by one they scrolled across the bottom of the screen and were confirmed. Voice commands would have been more efficient, but the Klingon system he had had to adapt to his own purposes did not have that capability, at least not with the degree of precision and reliability he required.

As the last of the commands echoed across the screen, the shuttlebay doors began to close. He laughed as he imagined the face of the shuttle pilot, and then Kirk's as the report reached the bridge. The captain would be beside himself! He lived for control —over men and machines alike—and it was slipping away from him, heading for anarchy.

A blip on the screen indicated someone had tried to manually override the doors, and he laughed again. It was almost too bad that Kirk would have to die along with the others. It would be so much more satisfying to be able to face him, to tell him precisely what had been happening to him—and why.

Another blip, another attempt at manual override. This time it was from Engineering, probably Scott.

For several seconds nothing happened. Then a whole series of coded commands and responses, each easily recognizable to his practiced eye, sped across the screen.

More tests, not of the sensors this time, but of the control circuits, the bypasses, even parts of the computer.

But not, of course, the parts that counted. Those were—

Frowning, he followed one of the data strings across the screen. He didn't recognize it. Was Spock's replacement better than he gave him credit for? Had he inherited one of the troubleshooting programs Spock had been working on and decided to try it himself?

But no, it wasn't a string indicating a test. It was a response—a response the computer had produced.

A response that the computer *shouldn't* have produced, he realized uneasily.

His frown deepening, he waited until the series ended. The tests were over, at least for the moment. To make sure they didn't start up again while he was doing his own, he tapped in a single command, then proceeded, sending messages flashing across the screen.

For five minutes they continued, his eyes scanning the patterns, recognizing and disregarding, recognizing and disregarding.

Until—

What was *this?* A chill swept over him. Had he made a mistake? After all those months of work, could he have overlooked something this obvious? He scowled at the keyboard. With voice control, something like this could never have happened. Was the whole project about to come down around his head because of this primitive Klingon technology?

But no! Looking it over again, he saw that it wasn't a mistake, couldn't be a mistake. It was far too complex for a simple keyboard error in entering the program.

But if it wasn't a mistake, what was it? And how had it gotten in?

The chill of apprehension faded, replaced by an angry determination to get to the bottom of the mystery. Had Kelgar been changing things without authorization? If he had—

This might be the chance he had been looking for,

Hargemon thought abruptly, a chance to get Kelgar out of his hair. If Kelgar, mistakenly thinking he understood the intricacies of the programs, had decided to change them, chances were excellent he had messed something up. And if there was one thing the commander wouldn't tolerate, it was someone messing up. Like Kirk, the commander came down hard when things didn't go right.

A faint smile flickered across his face. The commander had been absolutely livid when the message outlining the escape of Spock and McCoy had come in from Vancadia. Someone had made a mistake, and someone would pay.

And Kelgar had made a mistake here, in the computer, and with any luck, *he* would pay. At the very least, he would no longer be the incompetent assistant and meddlesome watchdog he had been for the past six months. Another might take his place, but not immediately, not until Hargemon's own plans were well under way.

So, what exactly had Kelgar done? Or, more likely, what had he *tried* to do? Smiling faintly, Hargemon began methodically entering commands and questions.

Slowly, as the responses began to flow, the smile faded. Whatever Kelgar had done, it was far more complex than Hargemon had expected. This change had been embedded in the very heart of his own program, affecting every aspect of it.

And it was well hidden, he realized with a start. If he hadn't spotted that one anomalous response as it raced across the screen, he never would have found it. Grudgingly, he upped his estimate of Kelgar's competence a notch. This was not the job of the bungler he had taken the Klingon to be. This was the work of someone who, Klingon or not, knew precisely what he was doing.

Someone who, Hargemon realized with a new chill, knew almost as much as he himself did about computers—or at least about this particular computer. But still, what did these changes *do?*

More questions, more commands, more responses streaming across the screen. Until—

"So *that's* it!" The words forced themselves past his lips.

The changes did nothing—as long as the *Enterprise* computer was fully powered and being operated.

But when it was shut down due to complete loss of power—as it soon would be—and its contents were read out by another computer—

"I see you've found it." Kelgar's grating voice came from somewhere, and a moment later his face replaced the data on the screen.

At the same moment, Hargemon heard something behind him—a hiss and then a click. Jerking around, he saw that the only door to the room had slid shut—effectively locking him in.

"What the hell do you think—"

"To tell the truth, Hargemon," Kelgar said, ignoring the other's attempt to speak, "I'm not surprised. And certainly not disappointed. I told the commander that you would very likely find it."

"The commander knows about this?"

"Of course. It was his idea. As was the alarm, so we would be alerted when you discovered the changes."

Abruptly, Hargemon stood up, turned, and pushed at the door. It didn't move.

"You will be unable to open it," Kelgar's image said.

"Why?"

"Because we couldn't be certain how you would react. After all, the destruction of one ship, commanded by a man you hate, is one thing. The destruction of all of Starfleet is another. Even a traitor like yourself might not be willing to go quite that far."

Suddenly, as he looked again at the Klingon's smiling—smirking—face, the situation came clear to Hargemon. Kelgar, in good Klingon tradition, was about to assassinate his immediate superior. He would put a different face on it for the commander, of course. But the commander would accept it and—

And the commander himself would soon be assassinated, and the credit for bringing the Federation to its knees would go to a *true* Klingon.

"You fool!" Hargemon snapped. "There is more to what I've done than you could even imagine! If you think that simply having my program infect the computers that will be trying to reconstruct the *Enterprise* computer's memory is all it takes, you are even more of a bungler than I imagined!"

"We shall see, Hargemon, we shall see. Or rather, *I* shall see. But I will give you a moment to appreciate my handiwork and perhaps revise your estimate of my capabilities."

In that moment, Hargemon's world, already listing badly, was turned the rest of the way upside-down. Suddenly, he realized that, whether Kelgar could succeed in his long-range plan or not, he could certainly succeed in carrying out its first step—the assassination of his immediate superior, Hargemon himself. He also realized that his only hope for survival, slim as it was, lay with the very ship and crew he had spent all these months plotting to destroy.

His fingers darted across the keys, racing through the coded commands before Kelgar could realize what he was doing and stop him.

But nothing happened. Where streams of data should have been racing across the screen, there was only Kelgar's image.

"You see?" Kelgar said. "The commander and I were right in not trusting you. If I hadn't set up those blocks to keep you from sending the reset code to the *Enterprise,* you would have destroyed our entire project before it had even gotten a good start."

Abruptly, Kelgar's image was gone. The *Enterprise* was back, its hangar doors once again tightly shut.

Hargemon's mind raced. Kelgar would be coming through the door behind him in a minute, possibly less.

Visualizing the screen the moment before the door had shut, Hargemon began entering commands. For once he was glad it was a keyboard input. If it were voice activated, he would have no chance at all. Everything now would be keyed to either Kelgar's or the commander's voice, and nothing he could do would open the door. But with the keyboard and his memory of the screen in the moments before the door closed, there was at least a chance.

Commands and responses streamed across the screen, until—

There it was, the exact configuration, including the command that had sealed the door!

He punched in another command.

The door opened. He wasn't dead *quite* yet.

Hargemon turned to the door—and stopped. He might be able to reach the remaining shuttle before Kelgar caught up to him. He might even be able to launch the shuttle.

But then all Kelgar had to do was return to the control room, set the ship on his trail, and shoot him down. He would never reach the surface of Vancadia except as dissociated atoms.

Unless—

Spinning back to the computer, he entered another series of commands, lightning fast. His heart leaped as he saw there had been no blocks set up here. The ship's navigation system was wide open.

Another series of commands, a half-dozen keystrokes, and Hargemon spun away, not waiting for confirmation on the screen.

Ten seconds later he was through the door to the ship's tiny shuttlebay. Punching the emergency door-open sequence into the keypad on the control panel next to the remaining shuttle, he leaped inside and pulled the shuttle hatch closed.

The hangar door swung up and the air rushed out. He was safe, at least for the moment. Luckily there was no convenient atmospheric containment field here like the one on the *Enterprise*. Kelgar couldn't get into the shuttlebay until the shuttle was out and the door closed behind it.

But Kelgar wouldn't waste time waiting for that. He would have heard or seen the inner door to the shuttlebay opening and closing, and he would already be on his way back to the control room, probably looking forward to the prospect of shooting the shuttle down almost as much as he had doubtless been looking forward to shooting Hargemon himself down in the computer room.

Taking the controls, he launched the shuttle through the outer doors the moment there was room, seconds before they were fully open.

Without looking back to see if his last-minute commands to the computer had done their job, he applied full power and accelerated toward the planet's nightside surface. There would be time enough later to worry about a specific destination and about how to find Spock and McCoy.

First he had to get out of Kelgar's range—and quickly.

Chapter Ten

"THERE *HAS* TO BE an explanation!"

Kirk paced the bridge in frustration. On the viewscreen, as it had been for the last half hour, was the surface of Vancadia, the shield still covering more than twenty thousand square kilometers and growing steadily more opaque. On the hangar deck, the doors stubbornly ignored all computer commands and all attempts at manual override, including those that Commander Scott had personally attempted on the hangar deck itself. At the communications station, Lieutenant Uhura had reperformed every check of her equipment known to Starfleet and a number that she had devised on the spot, and yet no response had come from either Starfleet Headquarters or any Federation starship since that one abortive communication from Admiral Brady.

"Aye, Captain, there's always an explanation o' some kind," Scott said, stepping back from the science station where he and Lieutenant Pritchard had together been trying to unravel one of Spock's special test programs, "but if ye' ask me—"

"I *am* asking you, Scotty, so if you have any ideas at all, please, *let's hear them!*"

"Aye, Captain, I was only going to say, I canna' help but wonder if we ha' not come up against another Organia."

Kirk grimaced mentally but gave no external indication. The same possibility had darted through his own mind with each new and inexplicable occurrence, but he had refused to dwell on it. It would have been pointless. If they had indeed encountered another group or entity with mental or technological powers even remotely approaching those possessed by the Organians, the *Enterprise* was in all likelihood helpless. The first—and so far, only—time they had encountered the Organians had been during another conflict with the Klingons, he remembered uneasily, a conflict that without the Organians' interference could have developed into a full-scale human-Klingon war. The Organians, however, when they finally lost patience with both sides, had simply and simultaneously disabled all Federation and Klingon weapons throughout the galaxy. Disrupting subspace links to Starfleet Headquarters would be comparative child's play for someone like that.

The similarities to the present situation were obvious, but it was equally obvious that until they knew for sure, they had to assume just the opposite. Assuming some benevolent superpower like the Organians was in control could be fatal if that assumption was mistaken. They had to assume, until and unless it was proven otherwise, that the responsibility for the current situation lay either in some so-far unexplained natural phenomenon or in something the Klingons themselves—or some new ally of the Klingons—had managed to accomplish. To insure their own survival, they had to assume that whatever was happening, it was something which, if they could only dig out the truth, they could combat or counteract.

"Anything's possible, Scotty," Kirk said abruptly, "but let's not roll over and play dead yet, just in case it's something else, something we have the power to deal with. Now, how are you and Mr. Pritchard coming with your analysis of Spock's program?"

He wasn't going to make it.

The last-second sabotage of the navigation system hadn't bought him enough time. Once again he had underestimated Kelgar. The Klingon must have realized almost instantly that the system was not working the way it should. It had probably taken him only another instant to realize the reason: last-minute sabotage by Hargemon.

In all, little more than a minute had passed before Kelgar had righted the ship, set it to relocating the proper coordinate system, and zoomed after the fleeing shuttle.

The first shot missed by nearly a kilometer, harmlessly converting its energy into heat and light when it struck the fringes of the atmosphere far ahead, but

Hargemon knew that the misses would not continue. The ship's navigation system, which he'd briefly locked on to a spurious coordinate system ninety degrees away from the proper one, had not yet completed its realignment. Once it did, once the lock-on was complete—in another thirty seconds at most—its radius of error would be down to little more than the diameter of the fleeing shuttle. And even if it weren't, another minute—or two, if he was extremely lucky—would bring the pursuing ship so close that Kelgar could make the kill manually.

Which, Hargemon thought grimly, the Klingon would probably prefer to do anyway.

Another bolt of energy seared the atmosphere almost dead ahead. The miss this time had been a few dozen meters at the most. The realignment was almost complete.

Abruptly, Hargemon nosed the shuttle over, sending it diving straight down. He wouldn't come down within a hundred kilometers of where he had hoped, but it didn't matter. This was his only chance for survival, to get inside the atmosphere before Kelgar closed in. Kelgar's ship couldn't enter the atmosphere, at least not very far, and the beams from its energy weapons, designed for the vacuum of space, would be blunted and scattered.

But then, just as he realized that even this maneuver wasn't going to save him, one of the massive surveillance ships appeared high up on his screen. Hope flared through him as his mind raced to recall the codes that gave access to the ship controls. But even as the first of the sequences began to form, as his fingers darted toward the first of the keys, the hope vanished. The codes could be issued only by the computer in the main ship, the one in which Kelgar was closing in on him. Given enough time, he might be able to find a way to circumvent the safeguards that blocked signals from all but that one source and take control of the lasers and turn them on Kelgar, but the one thing he didn't have was time.

No, the only direct link between the shuttle and the surveillance ships was the one that could be used to detonate the antimatter charges planted in all of them. "Just to play it safe," the commander had said. "I don't want one of those killers trying to shoot *me* down if something goes wrong and it decides not to recognize my safe-passage code."

It had been obvious that Kelgar had only scorn for such "human" precautions, but he had said nothing. And now—

Another blast of energy skimmed by the shuttle.

Without hesitation, Hargemon jerked the shuttle to one side and then upward, its engines straining, the force of the maneuver driving him down into the barely cushioned pilot's chair. He could hear the shuttle itself protesting with metallic creaks and pops. The edges of his vision clouded for a moment as he notched the force upward still further—and released it.

Suddenly, he was again in free fall. And on the screen directly ahead was the monolithic prow of the surveillance ship, its operating lasers presumably trained directly on him. But they wouldn't fire, he knew, not as long as the shuttle was putting out its safe-passage code. For an instant the thought of turning it off crossed his mind. If Kelgar was directly behind him—

But no, what he wanted was a chance to survive and strike back, not just a chance to take Kelgar with him. And his position, directly between Kelgar and the surveillance ship, gave him a moment to breathe. Kelgar wouldn't fire until he was clear of the lasers. With or without a safe-passage code, the surveillance ship would return fire if it thought it was being fired upon.

At the last second Hargemon jetted sideways, shooting past the surveillance ship at a distance of less than a hundred meters, then darting back in line with it, directly behind the massive rocket unit at its rear. If he was not completely hidden from Kelgar's Klingon-manufactured sensors, his image would at least be blended with that of the surveillance ship.

He sent the detonation code.

Behind him the antimatter pellet's containment field collapsed. Within milliseconds the surrounding normal matter closed in, and both matter and anti-matter were converted into raw energy. Like a minia-ture photon torpedo, the explosion took the surveillance ship out in a flare of heat and light thousands of times more powerful than anything the ship's lasers were capable of. Hargemon's rear-pointing sensors flared and failed, and the shuttle itself bucked, threatening to tumble.

Regaining control, he turned the shuttle's nose down again, heading straight into the atmosphere. Now at least he had a chance—several chances. If the explosion had come just as Kelgar's ship was passing, that would be best. Kelgar and his ship would be gone, vaporized in the multi-million-degree fireball. A little earlier, and the explosion would have burned out Kelgar's forward sensors, just as it had burned out his own rear ones. A little earlier yet, and even though Kelgar's ship might not have been damaged at all, there was still a chance that Kelgar had lost him in the explosion, possibly assuming he had been destroyed in it.

He would know within the next minute, when his shuttle penetrated the atmosphere—*if* his shuttle penetrated the atmosphere.

Chapter Eleven

THEY HAD SEEN only three moving vehicles within the city, and all were official government hovercraft such as the one they had commandeered themselves. One contained a complement of three, including a Klingon, but the others held only beings that Spock's tricorder registered as fully human. None paid the slightest attention to the stolen vehicle, but the one with the Klingon aboard, Rohgan noted uneasily, was just pulling away from the home of one of his fellow conspirators, another whose name Tylmaurek remembered from the pre-Delkondros Council.

"They must know *something*," Rohgan said with a nervous frown, "but obviously not everything, if they're checking up on people who've been at the ship for more than a day."

"Perhaps," Tylmaurek said, trying to sound more optimistic than he was, "they're just checking up on people I knew, people they thought I might go to for help. Perhaps that is why they came to *your* quarters."

Rohgan nodded. "We can only hope."

Then they had left the city behind them, and they all, except for Spock, breathed a sigh of relief. Even McCoy, though not letting his guard down, allowed himself to think that, just maybe, they would not be greeted by an army of Klingons at the ship.

Now the highway stretched ahead of them, even more deserted than the city streets. The only light was the faint glow from the smaller of Vancadia's two moons, shrouded occasionally by high, thin clouds. Not a single manmade light could be seen anywhere. It was as if the entire world had been shut down for the night.

"It wasn't always like this," Rohgan said as the last of the city's sparse lights vanished behind them. "I only hope, when your Klingons go on their way, the life will return."

For the next hundred kilometers—rolling hills and agricultural land that reminded McCoy of his boyhood Georgia—the two Vancadians tried to determine when the Klingons had first arrived in the Chyrellkan system. Within months of the Federation's initial contact seemed most likely, they finally decided, and neither Spock nor McCoy disagreed. The first rumors of Chyrellka's change of heart about granting Vancadian independence on schedule had started about then, and the first "timely" death of a political candidate had been only months later. The first time anyone heard of Delkondros was another year after that, and by that time Chyrellka had a new and almost hysterically anti-Vancadian Premier named Kaulidren. He promptly tightened Chyrellka's grip on the colony, taking power away from the Vancadians' elected government and giving it to the Chyrellkan overseers such as Governor Ulmar.

Then the deaths had started—the obviously violent deaths such as the ones documented in the tape that Kaulidren had brought to the *Enterprise*. Chyrellka had responded with massive numbers of arrests. "Sometimes they took the time to manufacture evidence," Tylmaurek said bitterly, "sometimes not."

The final straw had been Delkondros' ill-timed attempt to destroy not only the Chyrellkan space fleet but their ability to build a new one. From that point on, the Chyrellkans had become an occupying army despite the fact that the vast majority of individual Vancadians, like Rohgan, were appalled by both Delkondros' attack and the killings of resident Chyrellkans.

"In hindsight," Rohgan said at one point, "it's obvious that most of the trouble was purposely being stirred up by a relatively small group. A very ruthless group, willing to kill indiscriminately to achieve its goals. We—and I mean both Chyrellkans and Vancadians—aren't like that. Chyrellka had its wars long ago, but the planet had been at peace for two hundred years, had a working worldwide government long before establishing settlements on Vancadia. But those years made us naive. We believed what Delkondros and others like him said. We simply never thought—"

He broke off, sighing, and they continued in silence for several kilometers.

Soon the road swung sharply to the left, and the scent of salt air—sharper, cleaner than that of Earth but not all that different—touched their nostrils. Minutes later there appeared ahead the first artificial lights, aside from a few dozen isolated houses, they had seen since leaving the city. Skeletal towers, looking like miniature versions of the half-dozen launch complexes still preserved in the Kennedy Space Park, poked into the night sky above everything else. Spock's tricorder showed a concentration of lifeforms spread over several square kilometers, with perhaps a hundred in the immediate vicinity of one of the towers.

"Our only spaceport, now," Tylmaurek offered. "It's heavily guarded and, if rumors can be trusted, is being used primarily to evacuate Chyrellkan civilians and replace them with military." He shook his head. "Ten years ago the military barely existed. There were a half-dozen spaceports like this, bringing in hundreds of new settlers, even a few tourists, every day. Delkondros and the Klingons destroyed all that."

"Is your ship in there somewhere?" McCoy asked uneasily.

Rohgan shook his head. "Those are for the standard shuttle launches. Luckily our ship doesn't require all that support. With its drive, it can lift off from almost anywhere."

Slowing, Rohgan veered to the right, aiming the hovercraft at a break in the shrub-like growth that here lined both sides of the road. Simultaneously he boosted the power to the engines, and McCoy heard their muffled hiss increase as the machine went into its off-road mode and lifted itself inches higher off the ground. For minutes, then, that hiss was the only sound as Rohgan took them through a park-like wilderness of trees and grass and occasional footpaths, obviously little used in recent weeks. They were nearing the top of a hill, Rohgan maneuvering cautiously among the trees, when Spock, who had been studying his tricorder intently, looked up.

"I assume, Professor," Spock said, "the ship of which you speak is on a bearing of approximately fifty-seven degrees to the right of our present heading."

Rohgan shot a glance toward the Vulcan. "How did you know that?"

"There is a concentration of antimatter on that bearing. I assume it is your ship's power source. All the shuttles, now to our rear, appear to possess low-level nuclear drives."

"Antimatter?" McCoy sighed. "There goes the last hope that this drive—or anything else—was a legitimate invention. That antimatter had to come from the Klingons." He looked at Rohgan and Tylmaurek. "Unless Vancadia is capable of producing large quantities of antimatter . . ."

Rohgan shook his head. "Not that I am aware of. I know it is being created in laboratories on Chyrellka in minute amounts, for scientific experiments, but I have never been privy to the details of any of Delkondros' so-called inventions."

"Nor I," Tylmaurek added. "Whenever I asked anything—"

"Unit Seventeen," a static-shrouded voice called from a speaker somewhere in the vehicle, *"please respond."*

Spock immediately consulted his tricorder. "The signal is coming from the direction of the city," he said.

"I assume this thing we're in is Unit Seventeen," McCoy said, looking at the two Vancadians as the call was repeated. "Can either of you fake an answer?"

"I would not suggest it, gentlemen," Spock said, "unless you at least know the names of the occupants the caller expects to respond."

"But if we don't answer—" McCoy began.

"If we do not answer, Doctor, their suspicions will be aroused. If we answer incorrectly, they will be confirmed."

For more than a minute the requests for a response continued. When they finally stopped, Spock continued to study his tricorder.

After a few seconds he looked up. "Stop the vehicle, Professor."

"What? Why should I—"

"Our attempted subterfuge has been unsuccessful. Approximately five seconds after the caller ceased attempting to elicit a response from this unit, an electronic device began broadcasting a homing signal. I can assume only that its purpose is to guide the authorities to this vehicle."

McCoy grimaced as the hovercraft slowed and

settled to the ground. They were near the top of the hill, the trees thinning out. "Can't you find the thing, Spock, and remove it?" he asked.

"I have already located it, Doctor," Spock said. "I doubt, however, that it can be removed without adequate tools. It is approximately twenty-five centimeters directly behind the communication unit itself, and the tricorder reveals no way of gaining access. A most efficient design—most likely engineered to prevent hijackings such as this one."

"Blasted paranoid Klingons," McCoy muttered, "they think of everything."

"We're almost to the ship," Rohgan said. "If we move quickly, we can be there before they can send anyone after us. After all, we're nearly two hundred kilometers from the city."

Spock studied his tricorder for several seconds, scanning the area ahead. "That might be possible, Professor," he said finally, "but I suspect we will have some difficulty reaching the ship itself."

"What? Why should we have trouble—"

"We are now close enough to what I assume is the location of your ship for individual lifeforms to register, Professor, and two of the lifeforms in the immediate vicinity of the antimatter register as Klingon."

He had made it! He was going to survive after all!

The atmosphere, entered at a steeper angle than the shuttle had ever been designed to handle, had closed around him in a blanket of friction-generated flame, taking out his forward sensors and leaving him totally blind until the cocoon of superheated air cooled to transparency, and even then he would be limited strictly to what his own, low-tech but so-far-reliable eyes could see through the emergency viewport.

But he was still alive! It was, he thought with a sudden, silent laugh, at least a start.

The viewport finally lost its shroud of flame, and a patch of the planet's surface appeared in the narrow opening, barely visible in the pale light of the single moon. Still going down too steeply, he realized abruptly. Bringing the nose of the shuttle up another degree, then two, he leaned forward, closer to the port, in an attempt to get a wider view.

His heart leaped as he spotted, several kilometers off to the right, the lights of the shuttle launch complex. His luck was holding. The other ship, the one he had to reach if he was going to have a chance to ever get back off this world, if he was ever going to have a chance to get his revenge on the commander, was only a dozen kilometers inland and another dozen to the south. He was at least in the right area—a miracle, considering his method of descent. But he was also a long way from being home free. That other ship wouldn't be so conveniently lit up, and with the shuttle's sensors dead, he would no longer be able to home in on its antimatter.

But even if he could, he wouldn't be able to land there. He wouldn't dare use the decaying remnants of the nearly hundred-year-old landing strip. The

Klingons the commander almost certainly still had on duty there might not yet have been told what had happened between him and Kelgar, but even so, their inborn suspicion and paranoia would be more than enough to prompt them to notify the commander if an unscheduled and unexpected shuttle came careening in and the commander's right-hand man, who was supposed to be thousands of kilometers out in space tending to the *Enterprise,* came staggering out, suicidally insisting on getting on board.

And then there was the very real possibility that he was too late, that the ship had already been launched.

But there was no point in even considering such dire possibilities. If the ship had been launched, he would be stranded forever on this—

The shuttle lurched, almost dislodging him from his seat. Abruptly, his mind was again centered only on survival. What the devil had gone wrong *now?*

Jabbing at the controls an instant later, he saw what had happened. More than the sensors had been damaged during his fiery entry into the atmosphere. The tiny computer that operated them—and the shuttle's controls—was gone as well, some of its key circuits probably overloaded by feedback before the sensors themselves had given up the ghost. Damn Klingon design anyway!

Gripping the manual controls, he realized that Klingon design was *still* not through with him. The manual controls were designed for Klingon strength, not for that of mere humans. He could move them, but not with the speed or dexterity he would need in a situation like this, where split seconds could mean the difference between life and death.

Swearing silently, his eyes straining to spot familiar landmarks in the dim moonlight, he fought the controls. He was still fighting them a minute later, when the landscape seemed to suddenly leap upward into his path, and a huge tree—looking remarkably like a massive willow tree, a corner of his mind insisted on pointing out—thrust its drooping branches into his path and slammed the shuttle to the ground.

Chapter Twelve

WITH SPOCK'S ANNOUNCEMENT that there were Klingons at the launch site, all of McCoy's misgivings came flooding back. Rohgan, if not in league with Delkondros and the Klingons, must at the very least be their dupe. Either way, the activities of Rohgan's "secret" group of engineers and ex-councilmen must have been an open book to Delkondros, and he and Spock had never had a chance.

"It doesn't look as if you were very good at keeping a secret after all, Professor Rohgan," he said with a scowl.

"Considering the conditions we have uncovered, Doctor," Spock interjected quietly, "that failure is neither surprising nor blameworthy. In any event, it would be more profitable for us to expend our energies in an effort to plan our future course of action rather than in expressing recriminations regarding past courses."

McCoy turned his scowl on Spock for a moment,

then shook his head. "Logically, I suppose you're right," he said, "but I'm afraid I'm fresh out of ideas. And *almost* out of Klingon knockout shots," he added, tapping his medikit.

"If we could find another vehicle, one without a beacon—" Rohgan began.

"You're the one who said we'd have a better chance in *this* one!" Tylmaurek snapped. "If we'd taken mine—"

"Professor Rohgan," Spock interrupted, "are you knowledgeable regarding the physical layout of the launch site area?"

After a brief silence Rohgan turned in his seat toward Spock. "To some extent, yes."

"Then, if I were to pinpoint the locations of the two Klingons, you would be able to route us around them on foot and still get us to the immediate vicinity of the ship?"

"I would think so, yes."

"And are there any among those at the ship that you could trust not to raise an alarm the moment we approached them?"

"Several, I'm sure, although it would probably be better if there was some way I could have a minute or two alone with them before you showed your faces."

"Of course, Professor. However, we may not have that luxury. If—"

Something flashed in the night sky, a brilliant pinpoint that momentarily hid the single moon behind a light that rivalled a small sun.

"The ship!" Rohgan gasped, jerking around to

stare out at the fading light. "They've destroyed the ship!"

"No, Professor," Spock said almost instantly, "your ship's antimatter fuel is still on the ground, intact. The source of that discharge was . . ." He paused, studying the tricorder. ". . . beyond the range of this instrument to locate precisely, but the radiation is of a nature that could be created only by an antimatter explosion."

"Photon torpedo?" McCoy asked, his voice suddenly unsteady.

"No, Doctor. This was far smaller than any such device the *Enterprise* carries."

"But a Klingon vessel might—"

"That is a possibility, Doctor." Spock continued to study the tricorder. "And a small vessel has just come into range, descending along a trajectory that would be consistent with its having originated in the vicinity of the energy release."

"Klingon?"

"The readings do indicate Klingon technology, Doctor. The sole occupant of the vessel, however, registers as fully human."

McCoy shook his head. "What the *blazes* is going on? Tylmaurek? Professor Rohgan?"

"If it has to do with these Klingons of yours," Rohgan said, "you should be in a far better position to know than either of us!"

"If it continues on its present trajectory," Spock announced, looking up from the tricorder, "it will come down only a short distance from here."

"Land?" McCoy looked at Spock. "Or crash?"

"That is impossible to determine at this point. The pilot appears to have some control, but whether he has enough to land safely is uncertain. In either case, however, I suggest we investigate before making our attempt to reach the launch site."

"Spock, are you out of your pointy-eared mind! What we should do is make a run for the ship—now! If this thing comes down anywhere near, it'll provide a distraction! For that matter, that explosion has *already* provided one, and we should be taking advantage of it!"

"That does not logically follow, Doctor. First, it is possible that rather than distracting the Klingons and their possible allies in the vicinity of the ship, it has made them more alert. Second, it is also possible that they either know what the energy release was or were even responsible for it and have therefore not been distracted in the least. Finally, talking to the pilot, or failing that, simply inspecting the vessel or its wreckage, could contribute vital information."

McCoy rolled his eyes. "You can never have enough information, Spock, I know, I know. But there are times when you have to stop gathering information and *act.*"

"Of course, Doctor, and we will, as soon as we avail ourselves of this seemingly serendipitous opportunity." He returned his attention to the tricorder.

"Professor Rohgan," he said after a moment, "you may begin with a heading approximately ten degrees to the right of the launch site heading."

"That's where it's coming down?" Tylmaurek asked.

"That is where the vessel's present and somewhat erratic course indicates it will touch down. I would suggest, Professor, that we not waste any more time in discussion."

"Something we can finally agree on," McCoy muttered as Rohgan took the hovercraft out of idle and aimed it generally in the direction Spock had indicated.

Five minutes later, as they were topping another hill, a line of small flashes appeared low in the sky less than a kilometer ahead, apparently confirming the tricorder readings.

"That's not heading for what I'd exactly call a perfect landing," McCoy said with a wince as the flashes disappeared beyond the next hill.

"Perhaps not, Doctor," Spock said a few seconds later, "but the pilot has survived, though not without injury."

The vessel, they saw less than five minutes later, was small and utilitarian, obviously meant for a single occupant. It had plowed through the branches of the largest tree on the hillside. That was, in fact, what had saved it from even worse damage when it struck the ground halfway up the slope. Its single door had popped open and hung askew.

"The pilot is unconscious," Spock said as Rohgan lowered the hovercraft to the ground a dozen yards away.

McCoy cast a nervous glance in the direction of the

launch site as they climbed out. "What about those Klingons you spotted? Are they coming to look this thing over too?"

"It would not appear so, Doctor. Within the limits of the readings, they have not moved since they were first detected."

McCoy in the lead, Spock continually monitoring his tricorder for any indication that the vessel's drive or power source was edging toward an explosion, they hurried to the downed vessel. McCoy, his hand on his medical tricorder, reached it first and peered inside.

And froze.

"What the blazes—" He reached inside the cramped quarters with his medical tricorder but couldn't crane his neck enough to make out the readings.

"Spock! Give me a hand! This man is Starfleet!"

"Starfleet, Doctor?"

"He's wearing an ensign's uniform! Now, give me a hand! Let's get him out of here so I can do something for him."

As Spock paused to force the door open wider, McCoy continued to try to get some readings. Finally, the door was as open as it was possible to get it. Motioning McCoy aside, Spock reached in and managed to extricate the pilot from the seat, which had tilted forward but had not quite come loose from its fastenings. Blood covered half the pilot's face where it had struck the viewport.

As Spock lifted him out, the pilot groaned slightly.

"Looks kind of old to be an ensign," McCoy muttered, eyeing the short-cropped graying beard as Spock lowered the man to the uneven ground a few yards from the crashed vessel. Hunkering down, he began running the medical tricorder sensor over the man.

"That is because, Doctor," Spock said quietly, "he was once a lieutenant commander."

"What?" McCoy looked up, frowning. "What the devil are you talking about, Spock?"

"It is a long story, Doctor. What is important now is his condition. Is he seriously injured?"

Still frowning, McCoy turned back to the man on the ground. "Nothing broken," he said after a few more seconds with the medical tricorder, "miraculously. Lots of bruises, obviously some cuts on his head, and a minor concussion."

"How soon can he be returned to consciousness, Doctor?"

"Fairly quickly, Spock—if I had him back in sickbay on the *Enterprise*. But here, with no more than I have in my medikit, it would be a lot safer to let him come out of it on his own. Mixing concussions and drugs and very limited medical equipment isn't—"

"I realize that, Doctor, but I suspect this man may have the answers to a number of important questions, answers which conceivably could measurably enhance the probability of our safe return to the *Enterprise*."

McCoy was silent a moment, glancing from his medical tricorder to Spock and back. Despite his and

Spock's seemingly perpetual disagreements, McCoy could never bring himself, even in their most heated arguments, to doubt the Vulcan's knowledge or intelligence or even his intentions.

"All right, Spock," he said finally, "I know you're never inscrutable without a reason. Give me a minute and I'll see what I can do."

Taking a hyper-absorbent swab from the medikit, he hurriedly wiped away the drying blood from around the head wounds. He was coating the areas with the germicidal combination sealant and coagulant from the spray applicator when Spock looked up from his tricorder and briefly surveyed the surrounding landscape.

"Can he be safely moved, Doctor?"

"As long as we don't bang his head. But I thought you wanted me to wake him up."

"A matter of more urgency has arisen, Doctor. The Klingons I detected near the launch site are coming this way, apparently in a pair of hovercraft. Each also has an energy weapon and is accompanied by three other lifeforms that register as human."

McCoy grimaced but was not surprised. It was just one more indication that the Klingons were far better informed, far better coordinated, than Rohgan had thought. Once the beacon on the hijacked hovercraft had gone off and the Klingons back in the city had realized it was close to the launch site, they had probably contacted their launch-site counterparts and sent them out to collect the hijackers.

Or, more likely, kill them.

"How long do we have?" McCoy asked sharply.

"At their current rate of progress, approximately three-point-five minutes."

McCoy grimaced as he finished applying the sealant-coagulant and replaced the applicator in the medikit. As the doctor stood up, Spock slipped the tricorder strap off his shoulder and handed the machine to McCoy.

"I will transport him to the vehicle," Spock said as he hunkered down and slid his arms under the man's back and legs.

With seeming effortlessness, the Vulcan stood up, carefully cradling the man's head against his shoulder. Placing him in the middle of the back seat of the hovercraft in a sitting position, he climbed in himself and motioned McCoy to get in on the other side so they could together support the unconscious man. Rohgan and Tylmaurek were already in the front seat, watching Spock apprehensively.

McCoy, still tracking the Klingons on Spock's tricorder, climbed in. "It looks like they're trying to sneak up on us," he said, handing the tricorder back to Spock. "They've split up and are coming at us from both sides."

Spock studied the tricorder only a second. "Professor Rohgan," he said, "how much time is required to activate the ship and take off?"

"Running through the normal checklist would take—"

"Limit your estimate to only those essentials required for an emergency liftoff, Professor."

Rohgan's eyes widened in the near darkness. "I would think a minute, perhaps less."

Spock glanced again at the tricorder and then to the left and right. "The two hovercraft will be coming over that rise, Professor," he said, pointing, "and around that grove of trees in approximately one minute. I suggest you take the most direct route to the ship—if you feel confident that you can trust the majority of your co-conspirators to take you at your word, quickly, and help us."

"I don't know *what* to think anymore," Rohgan said, licking his lips nervously. His eyes darted from side to side, toward the spots where Spock had said the Klingons would appear at any moment. He let his breath out in a whooshing sigh. "But I don't see what other choice we have at the moment."

The soft idling hiss of the hovercraft increased sharply in volume. McCoy steadied the unconscious man as the vehicle went immediately into off-road mode, rocking for a moment before it stabilized and began to move up the hill.

"Both Klingons have changed course to take into account our own motion, Professor," Spock said a moment later. "They apparently are able to track our vehicle directly by means of the electronic beacon."

"I can't say that comes as a total surprise, Spock," McCoy muttered, but the Vulcan seemed oblivious to the words as he shifted the tricorder to scan ahead.

"How large is your ship, Professor?" Spock asked a moment later, his eyebrows arching minutely. "How many passengers will it hold?"

"I don't know precisely. It was made from one of the original landing shuttles, which had seats for forty. But the cushions had deteriorated so badly that we had to simply take the seats out and cushion the floor and walls. Or so I was told. I was also told that no more than twenty of us would be aboard when it took off."

A moment later they topped the hill and started down. McCoy's eyes widened at the scene spread out before them. Even in the dim light from the single moon, he could see the entire kilometer-wide valley, its bottom almost perfectly flat, its length—at least ten kilometers—almost perfectly straight. Down the center ran a long-abandoned landing strip, not unlike the ones the first Earth shuttles had used. On each side were hundreds of decaying buildings, all with a prefab look about them, ranging from massive hangars and factories to what must have once been houses. On a hill on the far side of the valley was a complex of dozens of power accumulator antennas, each tens of meters across. At one time they almost certainly would have all been aimed at a solar power satellite high above the planet's equator, but now only a few still looked in that direction. Most were sagging, all were rusted, and some had collapsed entirely.

And at one end of the strip, almost directly ahead, stood the ship, looking for all the world like a large, blocky version of the old Earth shuttles, except that the rocket nozzles had been replaced by impulse engines.

And the door on one side was open, a makeshift ramp leading up to it. A line of men and women were climbing the ramp.

"My God!" Rohgan breathed. "Talk about timing! They must be just getting ready to take off!" He shook his head. "But they *shouldn't* be. If the people we sent to warn them after Delkondros' broadcast—"

"There are fifty lifeforms, all registering human, either inside the craft or about to enter," Spock said, looking up from his tricorder.

"That's virtually everyone here, including those who came to warn the ones who came earlier," Rohgan said. "What the devil is happening?"

"That's what I'd like to know," McCoy grated. Glancing backward, he saw the two pursuing hovercraft appear at the top of the hill and start down the slope of the valley after them. "But whatever it is, it doesn't look good."

McCoy grimaced as Rohgan pushed the hovercraft to its limit racing down the slope. Whatever the Klingons knew or were planning, getting to that ship still represented the only real hope he and Spock had. The beacon made fleeing in the hovercraft impossible. And if they abandoned it, the Klingons in the pursuing hovercraft would be on them within seconds, and they didn't have even a phaser with which to defend themselves.

Suddenly, they were among the buildings. McCoy

winced as Rohgan snaked the hovercraft between two hangars, their decay even more evident at this range. Ahead, the last of the passengers had reached the top of the ramp. Stopping in the door, he looked back, apparently hearing the hovercraft's approach. Behind them the two Klingon hovercraft seemed to have slowed, making their way along other, wider avenues than the paint-scrapingly narrow one Rohgan had chosen.

The hovercraft lurched to a stop and settled to the ground only yards from the foot of the ramp. Rohgan and Tylmaurek were out instantly, Rohgan waving to the man at the top of the steps. "It's Jarlok!" he said over his shoulder to McCoy and the others. "He's one of the ones we sent to warn them!"

"Rohgan!" the man at the top of the ramp shouted down. "What are *you* doing here? The last message you sent—"

"Was a lie!" Rohgan shouted back. "I have sent no messages since you yourself left my apartment!"

"Then why did—"

"I'll explain later! For now, please, you must trust me! We have to get on board and start the launch immediately!"

"But the governor's broadcast said that Tylmaurek—" Jarlok began, but broke off, his eyes widening as he saw Spock and McCoy climbing out of the hovercraft, Spock cradling the injured man in his arms, McCoy again carrying the tricorder. "Are you their prisoner?"

"It's nothing like that!" Rohgan and Tylmaurek

were at the foot of the ramp now, starting up. "The broadcast was a lie! Virtually everything you've heard tonight—and a lot of what we've been told the last several years—has been lies!"

At the top of the steps now, Rohgan gripped the other man's arm, while Tylmaurek remained a step down, looking even more uneasy than Jarlok. "There *is* an explanation," Rohgan said urgently, "but unless we lift off immediately, I won't live long enough to give it! Whatever you've heard tonight about the Federation, Jarlok, it's probably a lie! What is important now—life and death important to all of us!—is that we all get on this ship and get it up before those—" A gesture back at the two approaching hovercraft. "—can stop us!"

"But the startup procedure alone—"

"Can be shortcut!" Rohgan snapped. *"Must* be shortcut!" For a long moment Jarlok's eyes seemed to search Rohgan's. Then, abruptly, as Spock reached the foot of the ramp, the man backed away, turned, and was gone.

Rohgan quickly stood aside, motioning the others inside. Spock, despite his burden, took the steps two at a time. McCoy, only a second behind him, jerked to a stop, suddenly remembering the Klingon—Spock's "evidence"—still stashed in the hovercraft storage compartment. But there was no time to get him, and besides, the way things were going, they would have all the evidence they needed. With a last glance at the hovercraft, McCoy darted inside the ship.

The interior was a barren, quonset hut-like cabin with some kind of thin cushioning on the floor and walls. Many of the people were already on the floor, gripping makeshift handholds, while others were lowering themselves. At the front was a bulkhead with an open door, beyond which was the pilot's area. The one to whom Rohgan had been talking was just inside the door, talking earnestly to the man in the pilot's chair.

As Spock lowered the unconscious man to the thinly cushioned floor, Rohgan closed and latched the outer door. Most of the people were watching Spock and McCoy with open curiosity, three or four with what looked like fear.

McCoy grimaced as he looked once again at the tricorder before handing it back to Spock. The Klingons were no longer coming after them. They had stopped their hovercraft a good hundred meters from the shuttle and were remaining in them, presumably watching and reporting and asking for new instructions.

"Rohgan!" one of the passengers spoke up, his eyes darting nervously back and forth between Tylmaurek and the three men in Starfleet uniforms and Rohgan. "Why have you brought these—these assassins here?"

Rohgan turned sharply from the door, now solidly closed. "The broadcast was a lie!" he said loudly. "Delkondros himself killed those men, not Tylmaurek or any so-called Federation assassination squad!"

A dozen voices erupted at once, drowning each other out. Rohgan quickly raised both hands above his head. "for right this minute," he said, shouting above the other voices, repeating the words three or four times until the others fell silent, "for right this minute, you will have to trust me. I know that some of you will find it hard to believe that Delkondros is a killer, but it's true, and there's worse to come, far worse. But right now, all that is important is that we and these men from the Federation, from the starship *Enterprise,* get into space. If we succeed, there will be time to explain and—"

"No, Professor Rohgan, that isn't enough!" a new voice broke in. The pilot, an almost skeletally thin blond man, had gotten up from his seat and was standing in the bulkhead door, scowling at Rohgan. "We have been getting one different order after another the last few hours—from you yourself, among others—and now you come dashing in at the last minute with three people your messengers told us only minutes ago were cold-blooded killers! I am not—"

"They are not killers!" Rohgan almost shouted. "They barely escaped with their lives themselves! The government broadcasts were lies! Please, you must—"

The ship shuddered, shaking everyone into a sudden silence. The pilot spun around toward the controls. The seat he had just left was empty, but a sequence of lights on the control panel was flashing. Charts and calculations were scrolling across the display screen.

Wordlessly, the pilot leaped back to his seat and began jabbing at the controls.

The lights continued to flash, the messages continued to scroll.

The ship continued to shudder—and then began to move.

The pilot jerked around to scowl angrily at Rohgan. "Another of your surprises, Professor?" he almost snarled.

Rohgan darted suddenly fearful glances at Spock and McCoy. "What *is* happening? *Were* you lying to me?"

Spock, the moment the ship's engines had shuddered into life, had returned to his tricorder. Now he looked up. "Your ship is being controlled by signals being beamed to it from somewhere in space, beyond the range of my instrument."

Rohgan and the pilot both stared at the Vulcan. The ship was now accelerating sharply, forcing everyone not on the floor to grip the handholds along the walls.

"That's impossible!" the pilot protested. "Remote control capability was not built into this ship."

"Nonetheless, gentlemen, that is what is happening."

"This ship of yours—this *Enterprise* is doing it!"

"No, gentlemen, the *Enterprise* has no such capability."

"But don't you sometimes wish it did, Mr. Spock?" A new voice jolted everyone into looking around for the speaker until someone realized it was coming from the vicinity of the control panel.

The pilot spun back to the control panel, jabbing at the controls, trying to shut the voice off. As he tried, the ship left the ground and veered sharply upward. "Who are you?" he asked, slumping back. "What are you doing to us?"

Spock looked up again from his tricorder. "The voice is coming from the same source as the signal that is controlling the ship," he said.

"Very good, Mr. Spock," the voice said mockingly. "May I assume you have logically deduced my own identity as well?"

"In your current incarnation, yes, Premier Kaulidren." A new outburst greeted Spock's words, but almost everyone fell silent as the Vulcan continued. "However, I have not yet determined your true identity."

"I wouldn't want you to die without knowing that, Mr. Spock. It's Carmody, Jason Carmody."

Spock was silent a moment. "Certain aspects of the situation are becoming clear, Lieutenant Commander Carmody. Starfleet has always assumed you were either killed or taken prisoner by the Klingons."

"I thought that information would be available in your data banks, Mr. Spock. And it's correct. I *was* taken prisoner by the Klingons after Delar Seven, along with most of the *Chafee*'s personnel, but since I was already a prisoner in a Federation starship brig, the Klingons were naturally curious. In the end we reached a meeting of minds, you might say. I have been progressing quite well ever since, far better than I would have fared in the Federation, don't you think?"

"It is understandable that you would find Klingon philosophy more compatible with your own than the

Federation's had been. As I recall, the evidence that would have been presented at your court-martial, all given by eyewitnesses from your own crew, would almost certainly have resulted in your conviction on charges of willful violation of the Prime Directive."

"It no doubt would have." Carmody's voice grew harsher. "Starfleet would never understand, never accept my reasons for doing what I did on Delar—but what I did was right. In some ways I was sorry not to have the chance to officially present *my* side of the case, *my* reasons." There was a mock sigh. "It's too bad that my timid friends back in Starfleet will never know the truth about this episode, either. But that would defeat the whole purpose, then, wouldn't it, Mr. Spock? But the fact that you know that I am responsible for your coming deaths, not to mention the imminent death and disgrace of Captain Kirk and the destruction of the *Enterprise*—and, eventually, the entire Federation—will help alleviate the pain of my disappointment."

A dozen other voices erupted around Spock—questioning, frightened voices.

"You will explain to the others, won't you, Mr. Spock?" Carmody went on. "As much as you are able to logically deduce, that is. I would do the honors myself, but I do have other matters to attend to, particularly now that my assistant in all this—Lieutenant Commander Finney—had to be disposed of."

Finney! Instinctively, McCoy started to turn toward the injured man, but in almost the same instant, he felt Spock's iron grip on his arm, keeping him from moving.

"Spock! What the devil—"

"What did Mr. Finney do to earn your disfavor?" Spock asked with uncharacteristic loudness at the same moment, drowning out McCoy's splutters.

"I don't have all the details, Mr. Spock," the voice said with a smile. "Suffice it to say that, like Starfleet itself, he didn't have the stomach for the hard decisions when the time came. If I have the opportunity to speak to you again, as I hope I will, perhaps I will tell you more, but truthfully, I doubt that I shall. And if I don't—I won't lie and say 'Live long and prosper.' I will merely say goodbye. Goodbye, Mr. Spock, Dr. McCoy. You will never know what a pleasure it has been doing business with you and your self-righteous captain, about whom Mr. Finney has told me so much."

Abruptly, the voice fell silent, the connection apparently broken. "It would appear to be safe to speak now," Spock said after a brief check of the tricorder.

"So *that's* what you meant, Spock!" McCoy exclaimed as he turned and, steadying himself with one of the floor-mounted handholds, knelt over the man they had brought aboard. "'Once a lieutenant commander.' This is Finney! You recognized him at the crash!" Of course, he must have escaped before completing psychological treatment. "But what did Kaulidren—Carmody—mean about disposing—"

McCoy's words were cut off by a gasp from a score of throats.

Alarmed, he looked up, his mouth still half open as his eyes followed the gaze of the others to the pilot's display screen. The scrolling messages were gone.

In their place McCoy saw the menacing bulk of an approaching surveillance ship, its banks of laser cannon trained directly on them.

Chapter Thirteen

"SAME RESULTS, CAPTAIN." Lieutenant Pritchard looked up from the science station readouts. "The program confirms the existence of anomalous sensor readings, but it cannot pinpoint them or determine their nature. I know it sounds crazy, sir, but it's almost as if the computer were deliberately *hiding* information from the program. If Mr. Spock were here, he could—"

"But he *isn't* here, Mr. Pritchard!" Kirk snapped. "Is there anything more that those of us who *are* here can do?"

Pritchard flushed at the rebuke but didn't protest. Of everyone on board, he knew, the captain must feel Spock's loss the most—and dared show it the least. "I can attempt to modify the program now that the analysis is complete," he said, "but I can't guarantee what the results would be without information regarding the program designer's intentions. It doesn't tell us *why* the designer wanted those specific things done, or what he hoped to learn from the results. Or even if the program in its present form really does what the designer intended. He *was* still working on it when . . ." Pritchard's voice trailed off uncomfortably.

Kirk was silent a moment, his features softening as the frown faded. "Understood, Mr. Pritchard," he said. "Do the best you can." Turning away from the science station, he punched up Engineering. "Mr. Scott, any luck with the sensors from your end?"

"Not a bit, Captain. The units we pulled and replaced ha' been disassembled near down ta the molecular level, and everything checks out perfectly. Whatever the trouble, it's not in the sensors—not these sensors, at least."

"And the shuttlebay doors?"

"Two o' my men are working to rig them so we can open them purely by hand, without even the hydraulics. It will not be easy, Captain. The size o' those doors—they were just not designed for anything like this."

"Understood, Scotty. Keep at it. Lieutenant Uhura, have you—"

"Nothing, Captain. All circuits still check out one hundred percent, no matter what conditions I subject them to. We just aren't receiving any signals, standard or subspace."

"Captain," Lieutenant Sulu broke in, "a ship has just cleared the shield."

Kirk spun toward the science station. "Details, Mr. Pritchard! Power, lifeforms, everything!"

"It *looks* like a rudimentary form of impulse drive, Captain, but that shouldn't be possible!"

"This must be the improved drive Kaulidren told us about," Kirk said, his frown returning. Even the most basic impulse engine was an order of magnitude more powerful—and more technologically advanced—than nuclear-powered drives. "How is this one powered, Lieutenant?"

"A small antimatter unit, sir."

"Antimatter? Didn't your sensor scan earlier show no evidence of antimatter?"

Pritchard blinked, as if just remembering. "It did. And this amount *should* have been enough to register."

Kirk grimaced. "Another impossibility, one that even off-world interference wouldn't explain. Where is the ship headed, Lieutenant?"

"Its current trajectory will take it into an orbit just above the orbits of the surveillance ships, but with impulse drive, it can go anywhere it wants within the solar system."

"Lifeforms?"

"Approximately—" Pritchard began but broke off as his eyes darted to the appropriate readouts.

"Something wrong, Lieutenant?"

"I don't know, sir," Pritchard said after a moment. Swiftly, he called back a series of earlier readings from the computer. "No lifeforms," he said, and then, frowning: "But I was certain, when the ship first cleared the shield, that there *were* lifeforms aboard, several lifeforms."

Kirk had come to stand behind the lieutenant. "And now nothing?"

"That's right, sir. And when I called back the initial readings, the ones I *thought* had showed lifeforms— there," he said, gesturing at the screen, "you can see for yourself. Nothing."

"Just the opposite of the antimatter that wasn't there but now is."

Pritchard swallowed. "Yes, sir."

"The lifeforms you thought you saw—human? Klingon?"

"I—I don't know. Human, I think, but I only saw them for an instant out of the corner of my eye, so maybe I just assumed—But if they weren't really there anyway, it doesn't matter."

"Perhaps, perhaps not. Is Mr. Spock's diagnostic program still running?"

"Yes, sir. I modified it to constantly monitor computer activity." As Pritchard spoke, he tapped in the code that brought up the diagnostic displays. "It shows basically the same as it has from the start, Captain. It insists there are anomalous sensor readings, but it still cannot identify or locate them."

"As if the computer were purposely hiding something from the program—isn't that what you said before, Lieutenant?"

"Yes, sir, but—"

"If that were true, then it could also be hiding the fact that there *are* lifeforms on board that ship."

"I suppose so, sir, but it doesn't make sense."

"Virtually nothing that's happened since we arrived

in the Chyrellkan system has made sense, Lieutenant, so that's not a valid criterion. For the moment assume it's possible. Then try to figure out how something like that could be done."

"Basically, sir, the entire computer would probably have to be reprogrammed."

"And anything that major would have to leave traces—huge muddy footprints, I would think."

"Normally, yes, sir, but someone who was really good—"

"Could clean up his footprints almost perfectly. Someone like Mr. Spock. Understood, Mr. Pritchard. And it would take someone like Mr. Spock to find the few traces that were missed."

"Yes, sir."

"Do the best you can in his absence. In the meantime, how is this ship being guided if there isn't a pilot on board? Remote control?"

"No, sir, there is no indication of external control signals. It must be following a preprogrammed path."

"Weapons?"

"No, sir."

"Then the surveillance ships will almost certainly destroy it."

"If they operate as Premier Kaulidren said, yes."

As Pritchard spoke, he had continued to scan the readouts. Now his eyes widened. "Captain! There *are* weapons! I could have sworn—"

"What kind of weapons?"

"Five laser cannon, sir. But they weren't there before!"

"Like the antimatter and the lifeforms?"

"Yes, sir, but I could have been mistaken about the lifeform readings, and the amount of antimatter was small enough that it could conceivably have been missed by the sensors in the earlier scan. But these weapons would have registered so plainly, I couldn't possibly have missed them!"

"The result of another 'anomalous' sensor reading, Lieutenant? Have you checked the record of the original readings?"

"Doing it now, sir." His fingers darted across the keys. As the readouts changed, he shook his head. "They were there, sir, right from the start."

"According to the computer records, Mr. Pritchard, according to the computer records." The faintest glimmer of an idea began to form in his mind. "For the moment concentrate all your efforts on working with the diagnostic program. Get whatever help you need." Kirk turned toward the communications station.

"Lieutenant Uhura, can I assume this new ship isn't talking to us?"

"Nothing being broadcast, sir, and no response to our hails."

"Captain," Sulu broke in, "two of the Chyrellkan surveillance ships appear to have spotted the ship. They're on an intercept course."

"Mr. Pritchard, the laser cannon on the surveillance ships and the ones that may or may not exist on the new ship—assuming both do exist, would our shields hold up against them?"

"Indefinitely, sir. If the power the sensors now show the weapons as having is accurate."

Kirk grimaced. "We have to take *something* for granted. Shields up, Mr. Sulu, and put us directly between the ascending ship and those so-called surveillance ships. I'd like a closer look before it gets blown away."

"Aye-aye, sir, shields up, impulse power."

The *Enterprise* surged ahead, sweeping down toward the fringes of the atmosphere, the ascending ship growing on the screen. Then, as they passed directly over it, they pulled up in a sweeping arc and leveled off in front of it, pacing it as it continued to drive into orbit.

Moments later the nearest surveillance ship swept onto the screen, bearing directly down on them. "Sensors indicate laser cannon primed and ready to fire," Pritchard reported, but even as he spoke, two beams lashed out from the approaching ship, their power dissipating against the *Enterprise* shields in a coruscating band of fire.

"Shields holding, Captain," Sulu reported, "but the second surveillance ship is closing in from the opposite direction. We may have to pull back and enclose the—"

Sulu broke off abruptly. Almost simultaneously, the laser fire stopped, and the surveillance ship coasted for a moment, then pointed its rectangular prow upward, apparently heading back toward its normal orbit.

"Captain!" Sulu said, his voice filled with surprise. "The ship is gone!"

"What happened?" Kirk snapped. "Was it shot down by the other surveillance ship?"

"No, sir, it wasn't shot down. It's just . . . *gone*. Vanished."

"It has its own shield? Like the one on the planet?"

"No, sir. It just vanished. As if—" Sulu paused, casting a quick glance over his shoulder at Kirk. "The only time I've seen anything quite like it, sir, was when I saw a Romulan vessel as it cloaked."

McCoy's heart sank as he watched the massive surveillance ship grow ever larger on the screen. Rohgan was standing next to the pilot, who was back in his seat, trying to get the controls to respond. Except for Spock, who still kept a constant watch on the tricorder, all eyes were on the surveillance ship.

"Has the device that's supposed to protect us been activated?" Rohgan asked sharply.

The pilot shook his head as he continued to work. "I don't know! Nothing responds to the controls here, so if it has been, it's the doing of whoever is controlling us." He turned angrily to Spock and McCoy. "Are you in league with Kaulidren? Is that why you are here?"

"Yes, I would also like to know!" Rohgan had also turned to face them. "I took your word for these things, you and Tylmaurek, but now—" He shot an apprehensive glance at the surveillance ship on the screen. "Are we about to be blown out of existence? Is that what Kaulidren meant about being responsible for our deaths?"

"I do not believe so," Spock said quietly. "I assume, however, that we soon will be destroyed, one way or another, unless we are able to learn precisely what the one you know as Kaulidren is planning."

"Whoever he is," Rohgan said, "he seemed to think you already knew, Mr. Spock. And he seemed pleased, not worried."

"I know a little and suspect more," Spock admitted, "but not enough to save us. Our only realistic chance of survival—"

He broke off abruptly, looking up from the tricorder to the screen. "A ship, possibly a Federation starship, possibly the *Enterprise*, has just come within tricorder range," he said, retrieving his communicator from his belt.

As he snapped it open, the *Enterprise* itself appeared on the screen, half blocking the oncoming surveillance ship. McCoy had his communicator out an instant later, but neither he nor Spock got any response.

"What the blazes is going on?" McCoy grated, shaking his communicator as if to jar it into cooperation. "That shield can't be blocking us *now!*"

"It isn't, Doctor," Spock said, returning to his tricorder. "The *Enterprise* shields are up, but they would not—"

He broke off again as the *Enterprise* shields flared

under the surveillance ship's sudden laser fire, but within seconds the firing stopped.

Seconds later the surveillance ship quickly reoriented itself and began a rapid climb back toward higher orbit.

"Maybe if they come *close* enough," McCoy muttered, returning his attention to his communicator.

"I do not think we can count on that, Doctor," Spock said, his eyes still on the screen, where the *Enterprise,* too, was rapidly shrinking. "They appear to be returning to standard orbit themselves."

"That's crazy! They just saved our skins when that thing tried to blast us! You saw it as well as I."

"I saw the surveillance ship fire, Doctor, and I saw the *Enterprise* shields deflect that fire. There is no indication they knew we were on board. In fact, their current behavior appears to indicate they are not aware of our presence."

"That's even crazier, Spock. They *have* to know we're here! Even if our communicators are blocked somehow, their sensors would pick us up! At this range, they'd even be able to see that a Vulcan was aboard, so why—"

The screen flared brightly, far more brightly than the wash of lasers over the *Enterprise* shields. Most gasped, and everyone's eyes snapped back to the screen. "It's firing at us again!" someone almost screamed, and suddenly there was a hushed silence.

"It is not firing," Spock said, looking up once again from his tricorder. "The nearest surveillance ship has just been destroyed in an antimatter explosion."

McCoy, abruptly giving up on making sense of anything that was happening, shook his head. Then his eyes fell on the injured and still unconscious man they had brought aboard.

"Like the explosion that went off just before our friend here came down?" McCoy asked, frowning in new puzzlement. "Is something shooting them down, Spock, or what?"

"The explosions were quite similar, Doctor," Spock said, returning once again to the tricorder, "but I suspect that they were not shot down. Another such ship has just come within range, and it, too, contains a small amount of antimatter. The ship's power, however, is derived from nuclear fusion. The antimatter is not part of a power-generating device but is isolated in a simple containment field. It is logical to assume that the first ship was similarly equipped and that its containment field was ruptured in some way."

"Why the blazes would a ship carry a chunk of antimatter around if it wasn't using it for power—or as a weapon?"

"I do not have enough data to form a logical conclusion, Doctor. However—" Spock broke off again, his eyebrows arching slightly as something new came up on his tricorder. "I now have new data, Doctor. The surveillance ship to our rear has just been destroyed in an identical explosion. This one was preceded by a signal similar to the signals that are controlling the ship we are on."

"Which means what, Spock?" McCoy prompted when Spock fell silent for a moment.

"It would appear, Doctor, that the antimatter was intended as a self-destruct mechanism that could be triggered from a distance."

"Does this mean," Rohgan broke in, "that the antimatter in *this* ship can be set off the same way?"

"That is doubtful, Professor, although not impossible. The antimatter here is part of the drive, not a separate item with no discernible function. The person to ask is ex-Commander Finney, here. Doctor," he continued, turning to McCoy, "the sooner you can revive him, the better our chances."

"Reviving him and having him die on us won't do us any good," McCoy snapped.

"Then be careful to see that he does not die, Doctor. I have the utmost confidence in your skills."

In the next five minutes Spock's tricorder picked up the energy flares from two more antimatter explosions, but McCoy barely noticed them as he worked with the injured man.

Finney, Kaulidren—Carmody—had said, and now that he looked at him more closely, McCoy could see that it was true. He could even see how Spock had recognized the man immediately despite the superficial differences. All but a faint touch of the red in his hair had been replaced by gray. The entire lower half of his face was covered with a close-cropped salt-and-pepper beard.

But the eyes had not changed. They had had a tortured look in them when he had been found hiding in the *Enterprise* after the failure of his plot to fake his own death and manipulate the ship's computer so that its record would falsely show the captain issuing the emergency order that had supposedly led to that death. And now, even with his eyes closed in unconsciousness, his face held that same tortured look, as if his reaction to the injustices he had always seen as being heaped upon him by his superiors, even as far back as Starfleet Academy, had finally become a permanent part of his features.

The man who even now thought of himself as Hargemon was suddenly awake. Instinctively, he flinched as the last images of the crash of the shuttle flashed before his eyes. A gasp escaped his lips as even that slight motion sent a pulse of pain through his head.

Where the devil—

His vision cleared, and he gasped again as he saw the face of Dr. Leonard McCoy, looking down at him with its usual frown. And behind him was Commander Spock.

And Rohgan and a half-dozen of the group the commander had been manipulating.

And overhead—

With a start, he finally recognized his surroundings —the shuttle! And from the feel and sound of it, it was already on its way! If they had gone too far—

Abruptly, he turned his eyes to the two men from the *Enterprise*. "How far out from Vancadia are we?"

"We appear to have achieved orbit, Mr. Finney," Spock said quietly, "but we are still accelerating."

Finney let his breath out in a whoosh and relaxed,

letting his body go limp on the thinly cushioned floor. "Then we have plenty of time." His eyes went back to Spock and McCoy. "You may not believe me right this minute, but I'm very glad to see you two."

"At this point, Finney," McCoy said, "why should I believe *anything* you say? How the devil did you—"

"We'll have the chance to catch up on old times later," he said, the old bitterness surfacing in his voice. Wincing, he struggled into a sitting position, then swayed to his feet. "That is, there will be, once I make a certain transmission. Doctor, if you would lend me your communicator?"

McCoy's frown deepened. "Why the blazes should I do that? What—"

Finney held out his hand. "Because if you don't, I will be forced to use this ship's communication system, which has no doubt been booby-trapped. And if I do *not* make this call—and soon—this ship and everyone on it will be vaporized."

Chapter Fourteen

KIRK SPUN TOWARD the science station. "Report, Mr. Pritchard."

"The vessel no longer registers on any sensor, Captain."

"Was the pattern the same as that of a vessel being cloaked? Or is this something different? And Mr. Sulu, take us back to standard orbit. I don't want an accidental collision with that, no matter what it is."

"Aye, sir."

As the *Enterprise* swooped back toward orbit, Pritchard recalled the series of readings to the display, studied them briefly, started to speak, then called up another series from the computer. "Computer, perform a detailed comparison of these two sets of readings," he ordered.

"The two sets of readings are identical," the computer's feminine monotone reported moments later.

Pritchard darted a glance at the captain, then returned to the display. "Repeat comparison," he said after a moment. "Since the ships in the two incidents differ greatly in mass and volume, it seems unlikely the readings *could* be identical."

"The two sets of readings are identical," the computer repeated.

Pritchard turned to Kirk. "You heard, Captain," he said uneasily. "The comparison was between the sensor readings taken during the moments it took the ship to vanish and similar readings taken during the cloaking of a Romulan warship. There should have been *some* differences."

"Agreed, Lieutenant," Kirk said, frowning thoughtfully. "No two events of any kind should produce totally identical sets of readings. But considering the problems we've been having with the sensors, can we trust the present set of readings?"

Pritchard swallowed. "I don't know, Captain." He glanced nervously at the readouts and back to Kirk. "Commander Spock's program indicates only that anomalous readings do exist. It has not confirmed that any specific readings—or any readings at all—are actually in error."

"Understood, Mr. Pritchard. Mr. Scott—"

"Captain!" Sulu broke in. "A surveillance ship has been fired upon!"

Kirk turned sharply to the main viewscreen. "Maximum magnification!"

"Aye-aye."

For an instant the screen was filled with the image of one of the menacing-looking surveillance ships, a molten-ringed hole where one of the dummy laser ports had been. Then it was gone, the screen momentarily flaring in overload, then backing off the magnification until there was a small, fading sun in its center.

"Source of the fire," Kirk snapped.

"Unable to locate a source, Captain," Sulu reported. "But it would be consistent with laser fire from the ship that apparently just cloaked."

"It fired without uncloaking? That's impossible!"

"For a ship using a Romulan device, Captain," Sulu acknowledged, "but we don't know that this *is* a Romulan device."

"Captain," Pritchard announced, "the sensors have picked up the ship again."

"It's not on the screen, Lieutenant," Kirk shot back. "Mr. Sulu, check your coordinates."

"Aye-aye, Captain." A pause of no more than a second. "Coordinates checked. Still no sign—"

Abruptly, the missing ship reappeared, not wavering into view the way the Romulan ship had when it had uncloaked, but snapping into existence, as if a curtain had been suddenly raised.

"It's back," Sulu said, a frown plain in his voice. "It appears to be on an intercept course with the second surveillance ship in the area."

Even as Sulu spoke, the ship vanished from the screen once again. A minute later it reappeared, above and behind the surveillance ship. The surveillance ship had barely begun its turn to bring its own laser cannon to bear on the attacker when it flared and vanished. Moments later the attacking ship vanished a second time.

One by one, the remaining surveillance ships followed the first two. One got off a single shot, but it was more than a kilometer off its intended mark. At least, Kirk observed with a scowl, the attacking ship now uncloaked each time it fired. That first time, when it had appeared to fire while still cloaked, was certainly the result of the still-unspecified aberration of their own sensors, which was almost as disturbing a thought as the possibility that the ship really *could* fire its weapons while remaining cloaked.

"Captain," Uhura reported, "incoming signal. Audio only, standard electromagnetic, not subspace."

"On speakers, Lieutenant."

Her fingers darted across the controls, and an instant later Premier Kaulidren's voice, thin and plagued with background noise, filled the bridge.

"—is happening? I repeat, Captain Kirk, what is happening? The data we are receiving indicates that our surveillance ships are being attacked and destroyed by a ship or ships that they cannot detect! Is this your doing, Captain? Have you gone over to the terrorists? I *demand* to be told what is happening!"

Kirk suppressed a groan. "The Premier is not my first choice of people to communicate with, but at least he's outside the *Enterprise*. Mr. Sulu, take us to a standard orbit around Chyrellka, so we can make this a two-way conversation and see if the Premier has any new ideas."

* * *

Half the people on the shuttle were talking at once, reacting to Finney's sudden announcement that they would soon be vaporized. While Rohgan tried to restore some semblance of quiet, Spock tried once again to contact the *Enterprise* with his communicator.

"There is still no response, Mr. Finney," he said.

"Of course not!" Finney said angrily. "You need the right code—my code." *Just like the Vulcan,* he thought, *to keep butting his head against an obvious stone wall rather than ask for help.*

"A code to do what, Mr. Finney?"

"Give me a communicator, and I'll show you!"

Spock studied him silently for several seconds. "Mr. Carmody," he said finally, "believes you to have been—'disposed of' were his words, I believe."

Finney tensed. If the commander knew that he was alive—"When did you talk to—to the commander?"

"Shortly before you regained consciousness."

"You didn't tell him I was alive, did you?"

"No, it seemed best not to offer him any more information than he already had."

Finney let his breath out in a whoosh of relief, then smiled faintly, bitterly. "But I should have known you didn't. We would probably already have been vaporized if you had. The commander doesn't like to take unnecessary chances. Now please, a communicator. Or if you still don't trust me, I could give you the code and you could try to use it. The timing, however, is an important part of the code, as is the quality of the voice that speaks it."

Spock was silent another few seconds, still studying Finney. Then he handed over his communicator.

"Spock!" McCoy scowled at him. Finney's eyes widened in surprise.

"Proceed, Mr. Finney," Spock said.

Finney nodded. "You always did know when to put your trust in something," he said reluctantly, "whether it's a person or a computer." Flipping open the communicator, he began to speak, slowly and deliberately, uttering a series of seemingly random numbers and letters.

After more than twenty, he stopped.

And waited.

Suddenly, a sinking feeling gripped Finney's stomach. Had Kelgar changed the code? But why? Hadn't all the other booby traps been enough? Why change the code itself when he had already cut off all means of sending that code?

Unless—

A dozen scenarios flashed through Finney's mind. Kelgar had planned to cut him out all along and had changed the codes early on.

Or the commander had intended to betray him from the start, as soon as Finney had designed the program and installed it. And was no longer needed.

Or during the escape, Kelgar had *not* been fooled by the surveillance ship explosion but had not wanted the commander to know he had allowed Finney to get away, so he had *told* the commander he had been "disposed of" and then changed the code just to play it safe.

But no matter what the reason—

Swallowing away the tremors that were threatening to overcome him, he began the sequence again.

Chapter Fifteen

FINALLY, THE PREMIER appeared on the viewscreen. His usual retinue, Kirk noted, was nowhere to be seen.

"Do you have any idea, Premier," Kirk began before Kaulidren had a chance to speak, "why we have been unable to contact *anyone*, either through standard radio or subspace, since you left the *Enterprise?*"

Kaulidren blinked. "Considering the rate at which your equipment was failing before you allowed me to leave, this does not surprise me. However, your minor difficulties do not concern me at the moment, Captain Kirk! To all indications, our surveillance ships have all been destroyed or disabled. If this destruction isn't your doing, I can only assume that Delkondros has gotten new help from your Klingons and is even now on his way here to complete the destruction he began four years ago! I demand to know what you are going to do about it!"

"What would you have us do?"

"My God, Captain, isn't it obvious? What more do you need? Surely this so-called Prime Directive does not require you to stand by while thousands of helpless people are slaughtered! Particularly when these Klingons of yours are obviously involved, perhaps even directly responsible! I heard your Admiral Brady say you had authority to—to do whatever you felt was required! Well, what is *required* is that that ship be stopped! It is almost certainly on its way toward Chyrellka right now. If its drive is similar to that of the ones that were destroyed during the initial attack on us, it could be here within hours! Its target—its *first* target—will undoubtedly be the same now as it was then: the orbital factory that manufactures our interplanetary ships. There are thousands of Chyrellkans there, both the workers and their families and more—thousands that will die unless you *do* something!"

"I suggest you begin evacuation without wasting any more time, then, Premier."

"Evacuation? Impossible! With our shuttles, it would take days, not hours!"

"We will help. If you will have everyone on the satellite gather in groups and provide us with their coordinates and with coordinates of locations to which they can be beamed, the *Enterprise* transporters can do the job in the remaining time."

"Transporters? Those machines that tear you apart and put you back together? I don't think—"

"Would you rather they die?"

"I would *rather* you removed the threat to them!"

"If all else fails—"

"If this is an example of how the Federation helps

its members, Captain, I can see why so few have decided to join! Even if the evacuation is a success, the *satellite* will be destroyed!"

"Premier, the coordinates—"

"As you wish!" Kaulidren's face twisted in angry scorn as it abruptly vanished from the screen. A moment later one of his normally silent retinue replaced him.

"I will put you in touch with Bardak," the man said stiffly. "He is the manager of the satellite. You can discuss your requirements with him."

And he, too, vanished almost as abruptly as Kaulidren had.

After the third try with the communicator, Finney swallowed nervously and looked up at Spock and the others. "It's not working."

"Perhaps, Mr. Finney," Spock said, ignoring McCoy's derisive snort, "you should take the time to explain the situation to us. Once we know precisely what you and ex-Commander Carmody and an unknown number of Klingons have been trying to accomplish here in the Chyrellkan system, we would be able to find a solution to our current problem that is not obvious to yourself."

"There *is* no solution if the code has been changed," Finney said, shaking his head, the familiar look of tortured hopelessness returning to his eyes. "There is simply no way of finding the new one. And without the code, there's no way to stop what's going to happen."

"And what the blazes *is* going to happen, Finney?" McCoy asked harshly. "And how soon? For that matter, I wouldn't mind knowing *why!* We *all* wouldn't mind knowing why we're about to die!"

Finney winced at McCoy's words. Under lowered lids, he saw the others, dozens of them, all watching him, fear and anger in their eyes. For a long moment the faces swam before him, anonymous and distant, strangers all, even the dozen whose names he had known for the last three years.

Until—

Without warning, one of the faces, one of the half-dozen young women in the group, leaped out at him. It was impossible, but—

"Jamie?" His daughter's name escaped in a harsh whisper from his suddenly constricted throat. For a blurred instant the shuttle vanished from around him, and he was back on the *Enterprise* all those years ago, his sabotage complete, his revenge about to be completed as Kirk's ship began its catastrophic fall from orbit.

Then he discovered Jamie was on board, brought there by Kirk to be destroyed. And now, somehow, he had brought her *here,* on this—this—

Violently, he shook his head, sending her imagined face and the dozens of others spinning away. He clamped his eyes shut against the sudden vertigo.

Hands were gripping his shoulders, keeping him from falling as the deck seemed to sway beneath his feet.

"Finney! Are you all right?" It was McCoy's harsh voice, grating on his ears.

Fearfully, he opened his eyes. The doctor's face was inches in front of his own, scowling. The others were once again in the distance, steady, not shifting and wavering as if in a waking nightmare.

The face he had thought for an instant was his daughter's was nothing like Jamie's. That had been delusion, he told himself, dredged up from those other nightmares that had never completely gone away.

But she was *someone's* daughter, he suddenly realized, and that thought brought a sense of reality washing over him, enveloping him more tightly than the momentary delusion had, more completely than anything in his life had done for years. Everyone here, everyone whose imminent death he was responsible for, was *someone's* daughter, or son or sister or brother!

All these faces belonged to real people. They were no longer just names and numbers in the plan—the game of revenge—he and the commander had worked out. Except for Kirk and his other enemies on the *Enterprise,* he had never had to face any of the anonymous people trapped by his plans, had never had to look them in the eyes and—

Swallowing, he looked up but still avoided McCoy's eyes. "One way or another," he said, "sometime in the next few hours, the *Enterprise* is going to destroy this ship, probably with its phaser banks, possibly with a photon torpedo."

"That's crazy!" McCoy snapped. "Jim would never fire on an unarmed ship full of people!"

"He won't know it's unarmed. And he won't know that anyone is on board."

"That's even crazier! The *Enterprise* sensors can pick up the bugs that digest your food. How could they possibly miss—" He broke off, remembering how, only minutes before, the *Enterprise* had come within kilometers of them and had acted as if they hadn't existed.

"The sensors won't miss anything," Finney said. "But the computer won't pass the information along to the crew."

"How the blazes could—" McCoy broke off again, this time in sudden comprehension as he remembered, once again, that other time when Finney and the captain had faced each other.

"You jiggered the computer! Just like you did when you set Jim up for a court-martial! But when—how—"

Finney took a coin-sized object from where it had been fastened tightly to his belt. He held it out toward Spock. "Let your tricorder take a look at this, Commander Spock."

"It emits a code that can be picked up by the computer," Spock said after a few seconds. "I assume that the computer's programming has been modified to recognize this code."

"I did it just a few hours ago, when Kaulidren—Carmody, I mean—I suppose I should get used to calling him that, though it won't be for long—when

210

Carmody was on the *Enterprise.* I was on the shuttle that brought him on board, in this uniform. That's why he refused to use the transporter, why he insisted on bringing the shuttle in himself, so he could park it next to a hangar wall to give me a better chance of getting out and back in without being seen. Once the guard Carmody left with the shuttle signalled me that the coast was clear, I slipped out and went directly to the main computer room. I knew the way well. I had the program on a data cartridge, so it only took a few seconds to enter it. Part of the program, of course, was the instruction to ignore the existence of anyone carrying one of these devices. The sensors would pick up my presence, but the computer, the split second it received the code this device broadcasts, would ignore it, would not even record the information in its data banks."

"And that's why the computer won't tell anyone that we're on this ship?" McCoy asked.

"No, this was only for my own use while I was within the *Enterprise,* subject to its internal sensors. My program has no control over those. This merely enabled me to get out of the computer room and back to the shuttle. It is the information from the external sensors, from the weapons systems, from all the systems that let the crew interact with the universe outside the *Enterprise,* that is controlled by the main program I put in. And that program is in turn controlled—monitored and controlled—by the computer in Kaulidren's—in Carmody's ship. And by the person operating that computer. We left a small monitor anchored to the *Enterprise* by a tractor beam. It acts as a relay station between the *Enterprise* and Carmody's ship. In effect, what the *Enterprise* computer shows the crew is what that other computer and its operator *want* it to show them. And all the while, the *Enterprise* computer will be recording, as it always does, everything that *really* happens, like the shooting down of this shuttle we're all on. There won't be any record of the relay station, of course, and once this is over, we'll be able—*Carmody* will be able to tidy up the records to his heart's content, until it's obvious to anyone with half a brain that the murders of Kirk's two close friends and fellow officers drove him over the edge, made him play fast and loose with the Prime Directive in his thirst for revenge."

"Dr. McCoy was right, then, Mr. Finney," Spock observed, "when he suggested that you have been manipulating the *Enterprise* computer in a manner similar to the manner in which you manipulated it when you staged your own death and attempted to have the captain blamed for it. Was that another reason for removing Dr. McCoy and me from the ship, to keep us from recognizing the pattern?"

Finney almost smiled. "You, Mr. Spock, yes. Carmody was afraid history might repeat itself, and he was probably right. You are the only one on that barge that had even a *chance* of figuring out what was going on."

"Do not underestimate the captain, Mr. Finney," Spock said.

Finney shook his head. "Oh, he may realize something is wrong, particularly now that I'm no longer the one in control, but he won't be able to do anything about it. Kelgar—"

Finney paused, grimacing. "Kelgar is probably the one controlling the computer now. I underestimated him in the past, simply because he's a Klingon, but now I don't know. He tripped *me* up easily enough, stabbed me in the back. In any event, even if Kirk realizes what is happening, there isn't anything he can do about it, not without virtually reprogramming the entire computer. Or stumbling across the exact code that will initiate the program that will return the computer to normal operation. No, this time there's nothing he can do. This isn't a simple little program like the one I used before. This one I worked on for almost two years. I'm not sure I could even find it myself if I didn't know precisely where and how to look. And even if I found it, I certainly couldn't undo its effects in the time that's left, not without the code."

"But *why*, Finney?" McCoy burst out. "What the blazes were you trying to *accomplish*, for God's sake!"

Finney winced again. *It seemed like a good idea at the time*, the old cliché darted through his mind. But now that he was forced to think about it, surrounded by his would-be victims, he was no longer so sure. The commander—Carmody—had been convincing and, he now knew, more than a little disingenuous.

"Kirk's the one who had you put away," Carmody had said, "the one who would have killed your daughter without batting an eye, just to save his precious *Enterprise*. And Starfleet backed him up, patted him on the back for betraying you, then and in the past. Just think of my little plan as a way of getting back at both of them, Kirk and his precious Starfleet. And we'll do it by using the very thing they try to live by, their precious Prime Directive."

The fact that he would be working with Klingons, that Carmody himself had essentially *become* a Klingon, in command of a Klingon team of soldiers and scientists, had not even been enough to dissuade him, not in the state he had been in then.

"Ability is what counts with us," Carmody had said, "ability and loyalty, not being slaves to a million petty rules—or to the so-called Prime Directive— that tie a starship captain's hands and keep the Federation from ever getting off its knees and becoming a force to truly be reckoned with—like the Klingon Empire."

And finally: "What do *you* owe the Federation or Starfleet, Mr. Finney? You were a better officer than any of them, and you ended up on the scrap heap! With me, with the Klingons, you will get credit for your contributions, not a psychiatric discharge and the humiliation of mandatory therapy, all for doing what any honorable Klingon would do, for seeking justice on your own terms."

And then, once he had been taken to the Chyrellkan system and given the Hargemon identity, he had simply been working on the program, out of contact with everyone but Carmody and Kelgar and a few of the Klingons. His mind had been totally occupied with the program, devising, refining, testing, over and over, until—

"The original plan," Finney said abruptly, "was to get Kirk—or the captain of whatever starship answered the Chyrellkan request for help in mediating —to fire on an unarmed ship, to fire on *this* ship that we are on. And that is what the *Enterprise* computer records will show that Kirk did. Starfleet will be humiliated, but more importantly, they will in the future bend over backward even farther to make sure they don't violate the Prime Directive *again*. According to Carmody, that will give the Klingons an edge. It will make the Federation even more cautious, more afraid to take chances than they already were, ripe for a Klingon challenge—a challenge that Carmody was planning to lead."

"So why did you bail out?" McCoy asked contemptuously. "Did you have a sudden change of heart?"

Finney shook his head. "I wish I could say I did, but—" Grimacing, he went on to explain how he had discovered the changes Kelgar—or Kelgar and Carmody together—had made to the program he had designed.

"They didn't think they needed me anymore, so I was expendable. The moment I discovered what had been done, I was as good as dead. But I also realized," he hastened to add, "that with those changes to the program, when another starship came to investigate and tried to salvage the *Enterprise* computer records, my program would be picked up along with the other information. And it would spread, to whatever computer the information was dumped into. In a few years, it could be in every computer in Starfleet."

"At which time," Spock picked up when Finney fell silent, "Klingon ships could enter the Federation at will, controlling what the Federation ships see, destroying them at their leisure."

Head down, Finney nodded. "I don't see what can stop them now."

Chapter Sixteen

LOOKING VERY MUCH LIKE a huge O'Neill colony, the Chyrellkan manufacturing satellite filled the *Enterprise* screen.

"How many, Mr. Pritchard?" Kirk asked.

"Approximately nine thousand, Captain. All but a handful have assembled at the specified coordinates."

"We'll have to ferry them down to the surface as fast as we can bring them aboard—the ship can't hold that many people. Start transporting, Chief," Kirk ordered. "I'll see what can be done about the stragglers."

"Aye-aye, Captain," the voice from the cargo transporter control room came over the intercom.

"Captain," Uhura called, "Manager Bardak is—"

"On screen, Lieutenant."

An instant later the balding official replaced the satellite on the screen. "What is it, Mr. Bardak?"

The manager swallowed nervously. "I'm sorry, Captain, but there are still a few who refuse to cooperate. They—they say they would sooner take their chances with the terrorists than with your transporters."

Kirk suppressed a grimace. "We were aware there were stragglers. I hadn't realized they were staying away deliberately. Keep after them."

"I will, but—isn't there some way you could pick them up anyway?"

"We need their precise coordinates in order to get a solid lock on them. Without those—there is one possibility, Bardak. If we have sufficient time, we could beam some of our own people to the approximate coordinates with extra communicators. Would your people physically resist ours?"

"I don't know, Captain, but I suspect at least some of them would. Even the ones who have assembled as requested are nervous. We have all heard of the malfunctions or sabotage your ship has been experiencing, so that even those of us who would normally not worry in the least about being transported—"

"I understand, Mr. Manager. But if Premier Kaulidren is right, the alternative is almost certain death."

"I know. I've explained that to them all, but it isn't enough."

Kirk sighed. "What about your own shuttles? Once we've beamed everyone else off, could your own shuttles transport these stragglers?"

"Of course, Captain, but there's no need to wait. Our shuttles—"

"No," Kirk broke in. "From what you and Kaulidren say, if your shuttles start taking people off, *everyone* will want to go that way and we'll have to start all over again. Keep your shuttles standing by, but—"

"Captain!" the transporter chief's voice broke in sharply. "Are you positive we were given the right coordinates for the people we're to beam over?"

"They match our sensor readings perfectly—don't they, Mr. Pritchard?"

"They do, Captain."

"Then something's wrong with the transporter, sir. I can't lock on to anyone. At those coordinates, my instruments show only empty space."

"Have you checked—"

"Everything has been checked that can be checked without tearing the transporter system apart, Captain!"

"Mr. Scott—"

"Aye, Captain," the chief engineer's harassed-sounding voice responded instantly, "two o' my men are on their way."

"Thank you, Mr. Scott, but I also wanted a status report on our shield generators."

"All operating at one hundred percent, Captain. Ta the best o' my knowledge."

"You don't sound all that confident, Scotty."

"Aye, Captain, I don't. Would *you?* Ten hours ago, I wouldna' have believed any o' this was possible, let alone all of it!"

"Understood. I know you'll keep on top of the situation." Kirk turned back to the screen, where Bardak's face still loomed large.

"What's happening, Captain?" the manager asked abruptly as Kirk's eyes met his. "I heard something about the coordinates being—"

"Is it possible you gave us the wrong coordinates for the assembly points?"

"I don't see how. I double-checked them just now, and—"

"Notify your people we apparently won't be able to transport them. Tell them to stand by, to remain at the same coordinates in case we get the problem worked out. Meanwhile, the *Enterprise* will move closer and extend its shields to enclose the entire satellite."

Provided the guidance system doesn't fail, too, Kirk couldn't help but think, *and we crash into the satellite instead.*

Everyone was silent for several seconds after Finney completed his account of his escape from Carmody's ship.

"How detailed was the analysis you performed that led you to discover Kelgar's changes to your program, Mr. Finney?" Spock asked finally.

"*Very* detailed. Otherwise I wouldn't have noticed anything wrong."

"If your code had been changed prior to that time, that change would have been included in your analysis, would it not?"

"Yes, I suppose so, but what could—"

"And the code itself could be determined from that analysis."

"Maybe. *If* we had a complete record of the analysis." Finney shook his head, a grim smile twitching at his lips. "I didn't have quite enough time to print out a hard copy to take with me."

"Perhaps not, Mr. Finney, but according to your account, you were observing the screen closely throughout the entire analysis."

"Of course! Otherwise—"

"Then all that is required is that we gain access to your memory of what you observed."

Finney blinked, then shook his head again. "My memory is good, but not that good. You're the one with the photographic memory, not me."

"You were able to reconstruct the data display that allowed you to find the command that opened the door for your escape."

"That was only seconds after I had seen it, not hours! And I had the computer to work with, to reconstruct the display and change it until I got it right!"

"Which you stated you accomplished in a matter of seconds."

A harsh, humorless laugh. "I didn't really have any choice in the matter, Mr. Spock."

"And you have none now, Mr. Finney, if you wish to survive. If you wish the Federation to survive."

"If you wish to survive the next *thirty seconds,* Mr. Finney, or whatever the hell your name is, never mind for the next few hours," a burly, middle-aged man said, stepping menacingly close, "you will do whatever you're told! Now!"

For the next ten minutes Finney wracked his memory, but to no avail. The harder he tried to concentrate, the harder he tried to build up the fleeting images of the computer screen in his mind, the farther the images seemed to retreat.

"It won't work," he said, slumping. "I can't remember."

"I warned you—" the same burly man said, but before he could say more, Spock had stepped between them, easily restraining the man.

"There is another possibility," Spock said, turning to Finney. "Mr. Finney, you are familiar with Vulcan mental disciplines."

"I know they exist, but I don't know what they are, exactly. I certainly couldn't learn them in the next two hours, even if they could conceivably help my memory."

"I am not suggesting that you do, Mr. Finney. I am suggesting that with your cooperation, your memories could be made available directly to me. Together, we might succeed."

McCoy turned on Spock with a scowl. "You're talking about a mind meld—with *him?*"

"Would you refuse him medical treatment, Doctor?"

"Of course not, no matter how tempting it might be, but—"

"Do not concern yourself, Doctor. The experience is never pleasant, so the nature of my partner is of little importance and could not, in any event, be allowed to inhibit my efforts in a matter of such urgency and import."

Spock turned to Finney. "Mr. Finney, I will ask you to not resist."

Finney shrank back. "I've heard about this telepathic trick of yours. You want to—to get *inside* my mind?"

"It is more complex than that, Mr. Finney, but you can think of it in those terms if you wish. Our minds will, if I am successful, blend into each other. Our thoughts will, under ideal conditions, become indistinguishable, as if our minds were one." Spock's voice was as calmly rational as always, his features as reserved, but as McCoy watched the Vulcan's face, he could see in the eyes—*thought* he could see in the eyes—a hint of the coming pain. The mind meld involved a total fusion of psyche, of self between two people, a breakdown of barriers erected over a lifetime.

Finney swallowed audibly. "Isn't there anything else you could try?"

"If there were, we would've tried it!" McCoy grated, then motioned to the burly man who had threatened Finney. The two of them took positions on either side of Finney, who darted looks at both men and then, pulling in a deep breath, closed his eyes and waited, his sweat-dampened skin suddenly tingling with an aching hypersensitivity that made the material of his uniform feel like sandpaper.

Unable to completely keep his rebelling body from trembling, Finney waited helplessly for his mind to be invaded. All sounds seemed to fade out of existence, except for the rustle of Spock's boots on the floor as he stepped forward, the sound of the Vulcan's breathing as he stood only inches away, and the pounding of his own heart as it forced his chest to pulse against the front of his tunic.

The sound of Spock's breathing stopped for a moment, followed by a deeply indrawn breath—and the touch of a palm on his forehead, the grip of the Vulcan's fingers on each temple and the crown of his head.

At first there was nothing but the physical touch, and Finney thought: *It isn't working. I'm safe. We will all die, but I'm safe.*

For what seemed like minutes, the same thought kept repeating itself like a litany while his heart continued to pound, his skin continued to ache beneath the sandpaper touch of his uniform.

But then, without warning, a wave of sadness swept over him, so intense that tears welled out from beneath his closed lids.

Not mine! his mind shouted. *Not mine!*

But at the same moment, he knew that it *was* his. *Now* it was his, something he had lived with and controlled and contained for most of his adult life, and he wondered how he had been able to do this without his mind shattering into a thousand aching fragments. But his mind *had* shattered, when his daughter—

No! That was another mind, another anguish, one that he had *not* been able to contain or control, even though he could see now that it was trivial compared to this other sadness that had come out of nowhere to drench him in its pain, but now they were becoming indistinguishable as Kirk's treachery became lifelong friendship and loyalty and then, a split second later, a new betrayal as the traitor/friend's face—the one image common to both pains—swirled before him, driving his thoughts into a kaleidoscopic mix of hatred and loyalty, unable to focus on anything else, until it was as if Kirk were physically there before him, about to betray/befriend him once again.

Jerking back, he felt Spock's fingers press into his temples. Unable to pull free, he could only stand and endure and wonder at the intensity until, finally—

A voice.

Out of that double pain came a voice, speaking slowly, precisely, somehow resisting that pain, rising above it even as he was drowning in it. With infinite stoicism and patience, it began guiding him backward from the present moment, back through his sudden awakening, the crash, the destruction of the surveillance ship, his escape from the commander's ship, his discovery of—

There! the voice said silently as the image of the computer screen wavered in the sea of pain behind his still-closed lids. *There is what we seek.*

Chapter Seventeen

STEPPING INTO SPOCK'S QUARTERS was like emerging from the transporter into an alien world. The sudden desert-like heat pulled an involuntary gasp from Kirk's throat, and the somber, red-hued lighting made it seem for a moment as if a translucent film of blood were blurring his vision. Normally, Spock kept conditions in his quarters more Earth-like for the convenience of visitors, but for the last few days, while he had been trying to coax the seeds of a cactus-like Vulcan plant to germinate—

In this "Vulcan-normal" state, Kirk realized as the door hissed shut behind him, the room gave a truer insight into Spock than anything else he had ever seen. More than the Vulcan's logic, more than his habit of sleeping with his eyes wide open, more even than his pointed ears and green-tinged blood, this room brought home to Kirk his first officer's non-human origins, his true alienness.

But it also brought home the Vulcan's strength and

dedication, not just to Jim Kirk but to Starfleet and the Federation. To Spock, the bridge—the entire *Enterprise*, except for this rarely used sanctuary—had been an alien world, its lighting harsh and overbright, its temperature chilling, its inhabitants illogical and often pointlessly savage.

And yet, knowing full well the physical and psychological environment he would have to endure, he had chosen it. And he had remained true, both to that choice and to himself, despite the pressures, both internal and external, to do otherwise. The constant pressure to "be more human," a pressure to which Kirk himself had often contributed. The neverending pressure, though unspoken for years, to follow the Vulcan way, the way Sarek had laid out for his and Amanda's only son. It would have been so much easier, so much less painful, both emotionally and physically, to have submitted to Sarek's wishes.

But he hadn't. He had chosen Starfleet, and he had risked his life in its service countless times. He had even risked his honor, something more important to him than his life, but *less* important than loyalty to those who had been loyal to him, all of which he had proven beyond any doubt more than once, but never more clearly than on that final journey to Talos IV with his friend and mentor, Christopher Pike.

Grimacing, Kirk wiped the sweat from his face and eyes. Why the devil had he come here? There could be nothing here that would help in their current predicament. Whatever diagnostic programs Spock might have been experimenting with on the terminal here would be as easily available on the bridge or at any of the hundreds of other terminals throughout the ship.

And Spock's special knowledge, his almost symbiotic rapport with the computer—that would certainly not be here. That was gone, gone with Spock. It was not something that could be left behind to be "absorbed" from his one-time surroundings, no matter how much Kirk wished it were possible. It was something that Spock had spent decades developing, decades of Vulcan discipline and self-denial. It was not something he could "will" to someone else, not even something that could be taught, except in its most rudimentary form.

No, he should be back on the bridge, where the current situation was displayed on the screens, constantly being analyzed in countless readouts. There was no reason to be here, sweating out his regret—guilt?—that he hadn't dug more deeply before allowing Spock and Bones to beam down. All it would have taken, he realized now, were a few of the right questions. He might not have been able to learn of the existence of the shield, but he would have at least learned of the other inventions and been aware of the possibility of off-world intervention.

"Captain!" The single word burst from the intercom, shattering his thoughts.

"Kirk here," he snapped. "What is it?"

"The rebel ship has just uncloaked, Captain," Sulu's voice crackled over the intercom, "and it's on an intercept heading with the satellite! No more than thirty minutes until the satellite is within range of the ship's laser cannons!"

"Keep our shields at maximum, Mr. Sulu. And Mr. Pritchard, get another reading on the weapons while we have the chance. See if there've been any changes since last time."

"Already done, sir," Pritchard's voice responded instantly. "All weapons readings remain the same. And still no indication of lifeforms."

"The missing lifeforms. Keep checking, Lieutenant. And keep Spock's diagnostic program running."

"Aye-aye, sir."

"Captain," Uhura's voice broke in, "the premier—"

"Wants to tell me again to blast that ship to bits," he snapped. "Tell him, unless he has some new information, I'll talk to him when I have the time."

Releasing the intercom button halfway through Uhura's acknowledgment, he blinked as the door hissed open, and the corridor lights, overwhelming after his minutes in Spock's quarters, almost blinded him. As he raced toward the elevator, the ghostly chill of moments before was suddenly and uncomfortably real as the twenty-degree-cooler air of the corridor evaporated the moisture from his saturated skin.

"What's happening, Doctor?" Rohgan asked. The Vancadian stood next to—practically right on top of—Spock and Finney, who sat slumped facing each other in two of the pilots' seats, silent and unresponsive. They'd been that way for close to an hour now, the Vulcan's hands cradled around Finney's head. "When will we know if it's going to work?"

Though Rohgan was trying to hide it, there was a note of anxiety in the scientist's voice McCoy didn't like. If Rohgan slipped over the edge and started to panic, he'd take the whole crew of the shuttle with him. That was the last thing they needed now.

"Now, Professor," McCoy said, taking his arm and leading him away from the two seated figures. "Spock will get us the information we need—it takes time to get that deep inside a man's mind, that's all. The main thing we have to do"—he raised a finger to his lips and simultaneously made a show of lowering his voice—"is make sure we don't break the meld."

Of course, McCoy thought, *how loud we are probably has no effect on the meld at all, but at least it'll help Rohgan stay calm.*

Rohgan nodded. "I understand, Doctor McCoy. It's just frustrating to sit here, helpless, with nothing to do."

McCoy sympathized with the man. He'd been forced to wait through the same thing more than once in his career—and to tell the truth, in this instance he was counting on Jim to come up with something almost as much as he was on Spock. He'd never heard of the Vulcan's being able to extract such a specific piece of information from a meld before.

"Then let's not sit around, helpless, and wait to die!" one of the shuttle passengers—a short, intense-looking woman—shouted suddenly. "Let's try and get control of the ship ourselves, turn it around—"

"With all the booby traps the Klingons have probably rigged?" McCoy interrupted, shaking his head. "No way. We'll just die quicker."

"There must be something we can do!" another passenger said in frustration.

"You heard Doctor McCoy," Rohgan said. "Our best chance—our only chance—is to wait for Mr. Spock to come up with the information we need."

"I say we take our chances on trying to gain control of the ship!" the woman said. "How do we know we can trust these Federation people anyway?"

"What choice do we have?" the professor asked, moving forward until he stood almost toe-to-toe with the rebellious passengers. "Listen to yourselves! Have you forgotten that we are scientists, that the very reason for this ship's existence is to prevent the kind of squabbling you're engaging in now?"

The woman stood silently for a moment, glaring first at Rohgan, then at McCoy. Finally, nodding her head, she and the group who'd gathered behind her retreated to the crew area.

McCoy glanced gratefully at Rohgan. "Thanks. I think you might have just saved my life again."

"You're welcome, Doctor," Rohgan said, nodding his head in the direction of Spock and Finney. This time, he didn't try to disguise the worry in his voice. "I only hope your friends can return the favor."

For what seemed to Finney like hours, the image of the computer screen in the commander's ship swam before him, too blurred by his newfound pain to be seen clearly, but held there by that other mind that, when he tried to examine it, was somehow also his own. Lines of code danced and pirouetted at the edges of his brain, too: memories of similar projects, his work of a lifetime ago . . .

And all the while, a voice kept silently after him, urging him to ignore the worst of the pain, to look more closely at the image, to *remember* what he had seen. Relentlessly, logically, it continued to hammer at him again and again, never stopping, never so much as pausing.

Until . . .

Abruptly, the image cleared. A part of his mind— *their* mind—was able, finally, to focus on it, to remember that if he *didn't* concentrate, *didn't* extract meaning from the shimmering screen of symbols, he—and all those aboard the ship with him—would die.

But this was an image of the screen from near the end of the analysis, he realized. If the information necessary to reconstruct the changed access code was anywhere in the analysis, it would be at the beginning, not the end, he thought and then felt himself agree.

The previous screen, that was the one in which he had finally discovered the nature of the changes Kelgar had inserted into the program, and he felt that other part of himself agree again, as if it were reading over his shoulder, not through his own eyes.

Slowly, an image at a time, he/they worked backward, each image seemingly sharper than the one before. A fragment here, a line there—Kelgar had hidden the changes well, had kept the code as simple as possible, so that a casual glance at the program would not reveal any alterations. Finally, they had all the necessary information.

But it had to be extracted, interpreted, and reconstructed. It would be like retrieving a handful of words from a sheet of paper, using an analysis in which the words were only one of a hundred elements being analyzed: the way the shapes of the letters were complexly intertwined with the chemical content of the ink in each letter, the way in which that ink reacted with the paper, the thickness and surface texture of the paper, and countless other details.

But the information was there, *had* to be there. Slowly, meticulously, he—they—began the process of extracting it.

Chapter Eighteen

WITH EVERYTHING CHECKED that could be checked, Kirk gestured to Uhura to put Kaulidren on the screen.

"What in God's name are you waiting for, Captain?" the image almost screamed the moment it appeared.

"We have your satellite within our deflector shields, Premier. They will withstand the lasers of the approaching ship indefinitely."

"But what if they *fail?* Your so-called transporters have *already* failed! Your subspace radio has failed! God knows what else has failed that you haven't bothered to tell me about! If you want to risk your *own* lives by relying on your obviously unreliable Federation gimmickry, that is your concern, but you are now risking *our* lives. Captain, there are more than *nine thousand men, women, and children* on that satellite! And you yourself said there was nothing on that rebel ship but weapons—weapons that will wipe out those lives unless you stop it, now!"

"We will keep that in mind, Premier."

"Do more than keep it in mind, Captain! *Do something about it! Before it's too late!*"

"I will do what I can, Premier," Kirk said as he gestured silently to Uhura to cut the signal. When the Premier's face vanished from the screen, Kirk punched up Engineering.

"Mr. Scott, any progress—on anything?"

"Not that ye'd notice, Captain," Commander Scott's voice came back, sounding decidedly ragged. "We've torn apart another dozen o' the sensors, but there's no' a blasted thing wrong with *any* o' them! And my men have checked the cargo transporter as far as they can without tearing *it* apart, and it checks out just as perfectly as the sensors. The only wee difficulty is, it *won't transport anything!*"

Kirk was silent a moment. "Don't start tearing the transporters apart, Scotty, not just yet. And don't replace any more sensors."

"Aye, Captain, but what—"

"We're obviously not getting anywhere checking systems after they fail, so let's start checking them *before* they fail. Monitor everything you can, as thoroughly as you can—shields, impulse engines, warp drive, everything. If something else *does* fail, and if you're watching it *while* it fails, perhaps you'll learn something."

"Aye, Captain, perhaps, but I wouldna' bet on it."

He still thinks it could be Organians, Kirk thought, but all he said was, "If there's anything there to be learned, Scotty, you're the one who can learn it."

Turning back to the main viewscreen, Kirk saw that the approaching ship was now visible in its center. "Any indication why it decided to uncloak now, Mr. Pritchard, instead of waiting until it was within laser range of the satellite? Power overload? Failure of some kind?"

"Nothing, Captain. But the sensor readings when it uncloaked were identical to the earlier ones—*and* identical to the readings from the Romulan ship years ago."

"And Mr. Spock's diagnostic program? Is it still reporting undefined and unlocatable anomalies?"

"Yes, sir." Pritchard leaned forward to study the ever-changing readouts. "It never stops. I've made a couple of minor modifications to the program, but—"

Pritchard stiffened abruptly. "Captain! A whole new series—they're everywhere!"

"Anomalous sensor readings?"

"Yes, sir, dozens of them! But the program still can't—"

"Captain!" Sulu broke in sharply. "The shields are failing!"

Kirk spun toward the viewscreen. "What happened, Mr. Sulu? Is it being caused by something that ship is doing?"

"There's no obvious relationship, sir." Sulu's fingers stabbed at a series of controls, his eyes taking in the results. "They're just—failing! No matter how much power I divert to them, they keep decaying!"

"Scotty! The shields—"

"Aye, Captain, I know. The power is still going to

the generators, and I canna' see a thing wrong wi' *them,* but the shields are decaying!"

"How long till they're gone entirely?"

"At this rate, no' more than five minutes."

"Do what you can, Mr. Scott. Mr. Pritchard, those anomalous readings—they coincided with the beginning of the failure of the shields, is that right?"

"It looks that way, but they've settled down now, to—well, to what I've started thinking of as a 'normal background level.'"

"Could you see any pattern? Anything at all?"

"Just that there was a flood of them all at once, sir. And when the program went back to look at them—" Pritchard shook his head in frustration. "It's like we talked about before, sir. The only pattern is that it's as if the computer itself were deliberately hiding information from the program. And just now—well, I know it's probably a misleading analogy, but it's almost as if the program saw this new string of anomalies out of the corner of its eye, when it had its attention somewhere else, and when it looked directly at the sensors involved, the anomalies were gone. Everything checked out perfectly."

"Except that the shields are now dying on us."

"Right, sir, the shields are dying."

"It *can't* be a coincidence," Kirk snapped. "Mr. Scott, did you see anything down in Engineering, anything at all, when this started?"

"No' a thing, Captain. None o' the monitors so much as flickered. They still haven't. For all I can see from here, the generators are producing the same energy as before. More, now that Mr. Sulu is tryin' to compensate."

Kirk shook his head in frustration. "What you're saying, Mr. Scott, is the same as Mr. Pritchard—it's impossible, but it's happening anyway."

"Aye, Captain, I could no' ha' said it better myself."

Impossible, the thought played itself back in Kirk's mind, *but it's happening anyway.*

And then, seemingly from nowhere, came a second thought: *Just as impossible as that other time, when the computer log showed that I had jettisoned Finney's pod while under yellow alert, when I knew I had done it only when we went to red alert.*

Suddenly, everything clicked into place.

"Captain?" At the helm, Sulu turned and stared quizzically at Kirk. "Did you say something?"

Kirk stared at the viewscreen, at the countless computer-driven displays everywhere on the bridge that flashed and flickered their messages on the status of every system on the *Enterprise.*

Messages he suddenly realized he could no longer trust.

"You're damn right I did, Mr. Sulu," he said, pushing himself out of the command chair. It was the only explanation—other than Scotty's Organians— that made sense. The planetary shield, the repeated equipment failures, the "anomalous" sensor readings Spock's diagnostic program reported but could not pin down—these were all "hallucinations" caused by something that had been done to the computer. Something that was still *being* done to the computer.

The sensor readings when that ship had "cloaked" —they were identical to those taken during the Romulan incident because they were almost certainly the *same* readings, pulled out of the computer's memory and replayed back through the sensor circuits.

The sensor readings that first said there *were* lifeforms on the ship and then said there were none, that there weren't weapons and then there were—they had been nothing more than "slips" that Pritchard had been alert enough to catch before they could be corrected.

Even that last, peculiar, interference-plagued communication from Admiral Brady could have been manufactured by the computer.

And the inability to open the shuttlebay doors, that made the most sense of all. The shuttlecraft sensors, unaffected by the main computer, would see things as they were, and that was something that whoever was behind this couldn't allow. But who . . .

It had all started with the supposedly false alarm in the main computer room, only minutes after Kaulidren and his retinue had come aboard in their shuttle. But it *hadn't* been a false alarm. There had been an intruder, almost certainly brought on board by Kaulidren, and that intruder had almost certainly sabotaged the computer.

Which meant that Kaulidren and the Chyrellkans

were involved, not just the Vancadians. Or possibly the Vancadians *weren't* involved. Those messages from Delkondros, Kaulidren's inflammatory evidence, none of it could be trusted, not now.

"Lieutenant Uhura," Kirk said, heading for the turbolift, "you have the conn. Mr. Sulu, come with me."

Finally, the last fragment of code emerged from the shimmering mass of symbols coaxed from Finney's memory, and Spock added it to the others. Spock was impressed by the sophistication of the Klingon programmer's changes—under different circumstances, he would have enjoyed speaking to Kelgar about them. At the moment, however, he had far more pressing concerns. For the entire time he had had to shield Finney, keeping his/their mind from being consumed not only by Finney's own shattered emotions but those that Spock himself had controlled and suppressed for decades. And those, unavoidably freed by Finney's invasion, experienced by their temporarily composite mind, had been even worse for the Finney portion of that mind than Finney's own.

Cautiously, Spock began to withdraw, but even as he did, he felt new shudders rippling through that other mind. When Spock's support was removed, its normal defenses, barely adequate to handle its own burdens without the aid of delusions, could crumble like an eggshell under the weight of what it had absorbed not only from Spock's memories, but from the objective look it had been forced to take at

Finney's own long history of irrational and hurtful behavior.

He would have to withdraw slowly, ever so slowly, trying to take as much of the memory as possible with him and giving the Finney part of the mind time to—

But he didn't have the time. No matter what happened to Finney as a result, he didn't have the time.

Bracing himself, trying to shore up Finney's own defenses as best he could, he prepared to withdraw.

Chapter Nineteen

BENEATH THE HANGAR DECK, in the midst of the machinery that operated the doors, a dozen men strained at the jury-rigged levers that Scott had come up with. With every connection to the computer broken, muscle power and leverage was all they had.

From the rear observation gallery immediately in front of a wedged-open exit door, Kirk and Commander Scott watched silently as, no more than an inch at a time, the hangar bay doors crept apart. Sulu sat poised at the controls of one shuttlecraft, ready to exit the moment the opening was wide enough. lieutenant Shanti sat in a second shuttlecraft immediately behind the first. Once Sulu was out, the Lieutenant would move her own shuttlecraft forward, anchor it just inside the atmospheric containment field, and wait, her radio tuned to the same rarely used frequency that Sulu's was set to. Whoever was in control of the computer presumably could listen in on any normal transmissions from the external shuttlecraft to

242

the *Enterprise* but not, they hoped, on communications between shuttlecraft. Even so, Sulu had been instructed to use the link only for routine communications. A set of signals had been arranged for specific findings—if the shields were indeed still up and operating, if there were or were not lifeforms and weapons aboard the approaching ship, if there were any ships present that didn't show up on the *Enterprise* sensors. Beyond that, if he discovered anything that might have a direct bearing on the state of the computer, he was to return to the *Enterprise* and deliver it in person.

"We don't know who or what we're dealing with here," Kirk had said as he had briefed Sulu and Shanti and the others in an isolated section of Engineering that Scotty had guaranteed was cleared of anything that could serve as a listening or observation post for whoever might be in control of the computer, "so we take only those chances that are absolutely necessary. And if you find something out there that will give us an advantage, don't take a chance of broadcasting it. If they know that we're on to them, if they know what our next move is, they might be able to counter it."

"Another ten centimeters, Lieutenant," Scott informed Sulu through his communicator, which was tuned to another frequency they hoped would be secure.

The only acknowledgment was the shuttlecraft lifting clear of the deck and maneuvering to center itself even more precisely in front of the opening.

Suddenly, the air in the opening shimmered.

"It's happening, Mr. Sulu!" Kirk snapped, though he knew Sulu had seen the shimmering himself. "Good luck."

Scott's eyes widened slightly. He glanced toward Kirk but said nothing. Until now he hadn't fully accepted the fact that someone was causing the malfunctions, but the failure of the atmospheric containment field at precisely this moment, apparently a last-ditch effort to prevent the launch of the shuttlecraft, could not possibly be coincidence. Both men took a step backward toward the door behind them. The shimmer increased, momentarily taking on an iridescent sheen, like oil on water.

Then, abruptly, it was gone. At the same moment, the air began to rush from the hangar deck into space, tearing at the shuttlecraft, threatening to slew it sideways and slam it into the too-narrow opening.

From everywhere around the hangar deck came the sound of exits closing and sealing, an automatic response to the failure of the containment field. Kirk and Scott spun and, facing directly into the outrushing air, struggled through the door directly behind them, the only one not already sealed. As they cleared the opening, Kirk kicked free the wedge that had held it open while Scott hit the override and sealed the door manually, insuring that Sulu and Shanti could unseal the door from the hangar deck side if it came to that. At all the other exits a dozen of his men were doing the same.

"He made it, sir," Lieutenant Shanti's faintly accented voice came from the communicator. "He lost a little paint, but he made it."

"Thank you, Lieutenant," Kirk acknowledged as he and Scott headed for the turbolift.

"Captain Kirk," Uhura's voice came over the intercom, "Premier Kaulidren wants a word with you."

Kirk and Scott exchanged glances. "What a pleasant surprise," Kirk murmured. "Tell him I'm on my way to the bridge, Lieutenant," he said more loudly.

As Scott exited at Engineering, Kirk simply nodded, silently mouthing, "Stand by, Scotty."

On the bridge, Kaulidren's image filled the screen. He was even more upset, and Uhura looked relieved to be handing the conn back to Kirk and returning to the communications station.

"Where have you *been*, Captain?" Kaulidren began the moment Kirk came within range of the screen. "That terrorist ship will be within range of our satellite in a matter of minutes!"

"There's nothing to worry about, Premier," Kirk said sharply. "Our shields will keep your satellite safe."

Kaulidren's face froze for a moment. "They are still functioning, then?"

"Of course."

The Premier was silent for several seconds, his anger seemingly on hold. "Then I take it," he said finally, "that you absolutely refuse to fire on the approaching terrorist ship?"

"Until we get certain . . . discrepancies cleared up, Premier, yes."

"Discrepancies? What is *that* supposed to mean, Captain? Or is that Starfleet terminology for 'malfunctions'?"

"In this case, it might be," Kirk said, putting a tone of reluctance into his voice. "However, as I said, there is no reason for you to worry as long as—"

"What discrepancies, Captain? What malfunctions? I *demand* to know! This is not some game! Nine thousand lives are at stake here! Now, what is it that you're hiding?"

Kirk glanced toward Pritchard who, along with Uhura, Sulu, Chekov, and a dozen others, had been at one or the other of the hurried briefing sessions with Kirk and Scott. "Anything new on the anomalous readings, Lieutenant?"

"Nothing, sir."

"And you're still positive about what you saw initially?"

"Positive, sir."

Kirk turned back to Kaulidren and the screen. "We have reason to believe, Premier," he said slowly, putting even more reluctance into his tone, "that there may be several passengers on the approaching ship."

"You *said* your sensors showed it to be unmanned! Or is that the malfunction you *might* be suffering from?"

"All I know, Premier, is that the initial sensor readings indicated there *were* lifeforms aboard, several dozen of them. Subsequent readings indicated none, but—"

"Captain! There are *thousands* of lifeforms on the

satellite this ship is going to destroy! Even if there *are* a few people on the approaching ship, they are obviously terrorists! They could even be those Klingons of yours, hiding behind some shield you know nothing about! You saw what they did to our surveillance ships—every one totally destroyed! And your own men—Captain, they killed your own men!"

"I understand all that, Premier, but until these discrepancies can be cleared up—"

"You're simply going to let my people be killed! Is that what you're saying, Kirk?"

"Of course not. We will keep the satellite safe inside our own shields for as long as it takes."

There was another long silence. "You are saying, Kirk," Kaulidren finally said, "that your shields are in full operation? Right this instant?"

"I already told you that, Premier," Kirk said stiffly.

Yet another silence. Then, suddenly, Kaulidren's furious scowl vanished. He laughed.

"So, Kirk," he said, "you know more than you're admitting."

"I beg your pardon, Premier?"

"Let's cut out the games, Kirk."

"You're the one who just now said—rather emphatically, as I recall—that this was not a game, that the lives of thousands of your people were at stake."

"True enough. Let me rephrase that." Kaulidren's eyes narrowed in a patronizing smile. "Your shields are *not* working, Captain Kirk. They have not been working for some time now. You know it. I know it. But here is something you *don't* know. They will not suddenly *start* working again, no matter what your chief engineer and his ham-handed subordinates do."

Kirk affected a deep scowl. "What the devil are you talking about, Premier? And where did you get this supposed knowledge about the state of our shields?"

"Please, Kirk, don't continue to play the fool. We both know it doesn't suit you. I don't know how much you've guessed, but it's a great deal more than you're pretending. But not nearly enough to save you."

"Save us? From what?"

"Disgrace, to mention one. And death, of course."

"Are you threatening us, Premier? I don't have to remind you, you're dealing with a Federation starship."

"I'm quite aware of what—and who—I'm dealing with, Kirk. You, on the other hand—but just so we'll be on an even footing, conversationally speaking, let me introduce myself: Carmody, Commander Jason Carmody, late of Starfleet, currently serving with a more congenial organization. 'Those Klingons of yours,' to be precise."

Carmody!

Somehow Kirk kept from reacting outwardly to the name. Until that moment he had been assuming the Premier was a native Chyrellkan working with the Klingons, but the sudden admission that he was instead a renegade Starfleet officer sent Kirk's mind racing. That Klingons on their own could have learned how to sabotage the *Enterprise*'s computer had not been easy to believe. But for Carmody to have learned the same thing—

But most of all, the purpose of this incredibly elaborate charade suddenly made a perverted sort of sense. Carmody, with the help of the Klingons, was getting back at the Federation for his own arrest, for the planned court-martial. He was getting back by trying to force a starship captain to violate the Prime Directive, just as Carmody himself had done, only on a more massive scale.

Hoping his face had not betrayed the thoughts racing behind it, Kirk widened his eyes in seeming puzzlement. "You're not a Chyrellkan?"

"You continue to play the fool, Kirk. I'm disappointed. Your Mr. Spock warned me I should not underestimate you, but these silly pretenses of yours make it increasingly difficult."

This time Kirk didn't bother to hide his genuine reaction. "Spock? When did you see Spock?"

"I didn't see him, I merely spoke with him." Carmody paused deliberately. "It was shortly after he and your Dr. McCoy boarded the ship I have been urging you to shoot down—the ship you *will* shoot down in a few minutes."

Swallowing away the mixture of emotions that were suddenly churning within him, Kirk scowled. "Now I know you're insane, Kaulidren or whatever your real name is! Commander Spock and Lieutenant Commander McCoy were both killed—"

"That *was* the plan," Carmody cut him off, "but they were apparently a little too alert for their would-be executioners. Not that it will save them for long. But to tell the truth, I'm almost glad they managed to escape, particularly since they ended up where they did—with a little help from me. I rather enjoy the thought that it will be you—or at least your *Enterprise*—that will actually do the deed."

Spock and McCoy were alive! Kirk could barely keep the smile off his face—but he had to, for the moment at least, in order to have a chance to save them. He snorted derisively. "Let me get this straight, Premier. You think that after what you've admitted, you'll still be able to talk me into firing on that ship?"

"Of course not, Kirk, and you know it. Really, your intentional obtuseness is getting tiresome."

No more to you than to me, Kirk thought, *but until I've given Sulu as much time as possible and learned as much as possible from you—*

"Then enlighten me," Kirk said, his tone still derisive and skeptical. "If you're going to force me to kill my best friends, I'd very much like to know how."

Carmody smiled in mock pity. "So that's your game, is it? You think that if I tell you what I'm planning, you'll be able to pull a rabbit out of the hat and stop me. Very well, I'll tell you, not that you haven't already guessed. I will do it the same way I shut down your shields, the same way I kept you from transporting everyone off the satellite. To put it in its simplest, most easily understood form, Captain Kirk, I control your computer and therefore your ship, and there is absolutely nothing you can do about it."

"Don't bet on it! Mr. Scott! Shut it down!"

"Aye, Captain," Scotty's voice acknowledged instantly, and at the same moment, all the screens, all the readouts on the bridge flickered.

And came back on.

Carmody's laugh filled the bridge.

After the jarring exit from the shuttlebay, Lieutenant Sulu quickly and efficiently checked the shuttlecraft's systems even as he scanned the immediate vicinity of the *Enterprise.*

The shields *were* down, the scanners showed.

And there—

In the shadow of the massive Chyrellkan manufacturing satellite, itself dwarfing the *Enterprise,* an object smaller than a one-man shuttle hovered, linked to the *Enterprise* by a narrow tractor beam. Was *that* what had its hooks in the computer?

Yes! Even with the shuttlecraft scanners, Sulu could detect a steady stream of data going both ways between the object and the *Enterprise.* For an instant he thought of simply ramming the object, even if the impact would wreck the shuttlecraft as well. His emergency field effect suit would keep him alive and well until the *Enterprise,* with its computer restored, could bring him in. And even if it couldn't, one life was a small price to pay for—

But there was more, he suddenly realized. A second stream of data was flowing between the object and something else, something beyond the range of the shuttlecraft's scanners. This tiny object was obviously a relay station. Possibly it was a vital link, but just as possibly it was a mere convenience. And even if he were able to totally destroy it, whoever was at the other end of that second stream of data would know about it. And would, in all probability, simply move closer and take over directly, bypassing the relay. And Sulu would be of no use to the *Enterprise* in a disabled shuttlecraft.

No, as a last resort he might attempt to ram the object, but for now, gathering information was more important. The ship Kaulidren wanted destroyed was still more than twenty minutes away, and learning its true nature was another of his top priorities. Kirk would already know that the *Enterprise* shields were down, since the absence of a specific signal to Lieutenant Shanti would have told him that.

First, a run to the approaching ship, and then, depending on what he found there, either back to the *Enterprise* with the information or out along that second data stream to see whatever there was to see.

Orienting the shuttlecraft, Sulu applied full impulse power.

Chapter Twenty

"Do YOU HAVE any more tricks up your sleeve, Captain?" Carmody asked, an arrogant smile frozen on his face.

"I assure you," Kirk snapped, "you'll be the first to know!"

"I have no doubt of that. But under the circumstances, isn't there something *you* would like to know? You were full of questions just a moment ago. Don't tell me your curiosity has been so easily satisfied."

"You obviously enjoy gloating, whoever you are, so go ahead while you have the chance."

Carmody shrugged. "As a matter of fact, I do enjoy it. But, then, who wouldn't, given such a perfect opportunity? My only regret, now that I've come to know you so well these last few hours, is that you will have such a short time to appreciate the situation. But the rest of Starfleet will have more, I assure you, perhaps as much as two years. I estimate it will take about that long to infect all your Starfleet computers. During that time you will be remembered as the captain who disgraced the Federation by violating the Prime Directive even more grossly than I. You will have fired on and destroyed an unarmed ship full of emissaries of peace."

Kirk interrupted. "You're planning to take on all of Starfleet? Surely you can't imagine this 'bug' of yours will go undetected—and uncorrected—for that long, in that many ships!"

"But of course it will, Captain. This was merely a test run, and despite some minor problems—which will of course be corrected—it has been a resounding success. In the future, even a program like your Mr. Spock's won't notice anything amiss. And once everything is in place—" Carmody paused, his smile broadening even more. "As an old Earth saying has it, Captain, it will be like shooting fish in a barrel."

"If you think you're going to get away with this—"

"I *know* I am, Captain. And *you* will know it in roughly three minutes, when your phasers begin firing. Now if you will excuse me, I have things to attend to."

Abruptly, Carmody's image vanished from the screen, replaced by that of the approaching ship, the ports for its laser cannon clear on its prow.

But a moment later the ports were gone, the prow smooth and unbroken. Another moment, and the ship melted into a totally different shape, a quarter of its original size. Even though Kirk had been expecting it, it was still unsettling. He tensed, waiting for the next sign. He didn't dare rush it, didn't dare play his one remaining card too soon.

"Captain!" Ensign Sparer, Sulu's replacement at

the helm, called. "All phaser banks are locking on to the approaching ship! Nothing I do has any effect!"

"All right, then," Kirk said, the beginnings of a smile forming on his lips. *"Now,* Mr. Scott!"

There was no acknowledgment, but an instant later, as Scotty and a dozen of his men at key points around the ship acted, the screens and readouts went out.

And this time they didn't come back on.

Spock staggered for an instant as he completed the mental withdrawal, pulling his hand back from Finney's forehead. Finney gasped and would have fallen, were it not for McCoy's hands on his shoulders.

"The information, Spock—did you get it?" McCoy asked, his eyes still on Finney.

"I believe I did, Doctor." Quickly he took his communicator from his belt and flipped it open as he eyed McCoy easing Finney to the floor. "Fortunately, the altered code does not appear to be keyed to any specific voice."

Slowly, then, he pulled the numbers from his memory and spoke them into the communicator while McCoy and the others watched and waited tensely. On the screen above the pilot's chair, the dot in its center had finally resolved itself into a tiny cylinder, a toy-like vision of the Chyrellkan satellite. A nearby dot was still just that—a dot, not identifiable as a starship, though everyone assumed it was the *Enterprise.*

Finally, after more than two dozen numbers, Spock fell silent.

For at least a half minute there was total silence, except for fifty people's breathing and the creaks and groans of the ship as it continued to be subjected to the unaccustomed stress of its recently installed impulse engines.

"Something wrong, Spock?" McCoy finally asked.

"The *Enterprise* computer is not responding."

"I guessed *that* much, Spock! Do you have any idea *why* it isn't responding? Could you have gotten a number wrong? Out of sequence? Are we out of communicator range?"

Spock was silent a moment, looking at the gradually expanding images on the pilot's screen. "It is possible we are out of range. I will repeat the sequence."

And he did, not once but a half-dozen times as the images continued to grow, though not as rapidly as before. Their ship was obviously slowing for its rendezvous with the satellite.

By that time McCoy had Finney back, if not to normal, at least to a functional state. "Do *you* have any ideas?" McCoy asked with a scowl as the ex-Starfleet officer lurched unsteadily to his feet.

Finney shook his head, not in a negative response but as if to clear it. "About what? What happened?"

"That new code that Spock extracted from your mind," McCoy said, "it doesn't work."

Finney looked blank for a second, as if the words took that much time to get through whatever barriers his assaulted mind had set up. Then he grimaced. "I was afraid of that," he said.

"Of what?" McCoy grated. "Come on, Finney, if you knew that code was no good—"

"I didn't know *anything*," he said defensively. "It's just that if Kelgar knew—or even suspected—that I survived that surveillance ship blast, he may've changed it *again*. Or if one of you," he went on, his voice suddenly accusatory, "said something to the commander that let him know I was here—"

"We didn't!" McCoy snapped.

"Attempting to assign blame is pointless, Doctor. For the moment I suggest that one of us continue to transmit the code in the hope that there is some other explanation for its lack of success thus far."

McCoy turned his scowl on Spock. "Maybe you should go back in there and check again. Isn't it possible your imperfect human half missed something?"

"Anything is possible, Doctor. However—"

"What's *that?*" The burly man who had helped McCoy restrain Finney was pointing at the pilot's viewscreen.

McCoy looked sharply toward the screen, his scowl changing to a sudden grin as his eyes focussed on the image.

"A shuttlecraft!" he exulted, throwing a scornful glance at Finney as he flipped open his own communicator. "Shuttlecraft, this is Dr. McCoy! What the devil is going on? And can *you* get a message through to the *Enterprise?*"

There was a long silence as the shuttlecraft coasted

to a stop in the viewscreen, its bulk entirely blocking the distant satellite and starship.

"Shuttlecraft!" McCoy repeated. "Answer me, blast it!"

He jerked around to face Finney. "You don't need that code to get through to a *shuttlecraft*, do you?"

Finney shook his head. "No, only the *Enterprise*'s computer is affected. The shuttlecraft are—"

"Dr. McCoy?" Sulu's startled voice came over the communicator. "Is that really you?"

"Of course it's me! Sulu, is that you?"

"Yes, Doctor, but—is Spock with you?"

"Yes, Lieutenant! Look, Sulu, can you get word—"

"If you really are Dr. McCoy, what is your daughter's name?" Sulu asked.

"Blast it, Sulu, don't waste time—"

"For various reasons, Doctor, I must verify your identity. Please, your daughter's name."

"Joanna! Now what—"

"But that information would be available in the ship's computer," Sulu said, as if just realizing it himself. "I'm sorry, something else—Dr. McCoy, the time you and Scotty and I dragged Mr. Spock to those old-time bowling lanes at Starbase Two—do you remember what you accused him of doing?"

"How the devil should I remember *that?* That was years ago, and I've accused him of everything in the book!"

"If it will facilitate matters, Mr. Sulu," Spock said into his own communicator, "the incident occurred at Starbase One, not Two, and Dr. McCoy accused me of deliberately setting up a seven-ten split in order to make the game more challenging. For some reason you found his accusation most amusing. Now, if you are satisfied with our identities, we have an urgent message that must be communicated to the *Enterprise* computer. We have been unable to make contact through our communicators."

"That's probably because the computer is shut down. At least, I assume it is by now." All suspicion was gone from Sulu's voice, replaced by a mixture of relief and urgency. "The captain suspects the entire system has been sabotaged."

"The captain is correct, Mr. Sulu," Spock interrupted. "But we now have a code that may allow us to reverse the effects of the sabotage if the computer can be turned back on. However, we must be able to contact the *Enterprise* before the code can be entered into the computer."

There was a startled silence, and then Sulu said: "Give me the code, Mr. Spock, and I'll return to the *Enterprise* with it and give it to the captain. We have a special communications link set up."

"Could you not broadcast it from here?"

"I could, but we're afraid that whoever is in control of the computer will be listening in despite our precautions. If they heard me giving the captain the code, they might be able to do something else to stop him."

"Mr. Finney," Spock said, turning toward the man, "is that possible?"

Finney swallowed nervously. "It's possible, yes. If

the commander or Kelgar knows the computer is about to be turned on and that the access code will be entered immediately, there's an abort sequence that he could enter any time before the code has been completely entered. There's no way of blocking it. It wouldn't give him control of the computer again, but it *would* make it essentially useless, wiping out all memory and programs. Unless," he added, averting his eyes, "Kelgar has changed that too."

"Thank you, Mr. Finney. Mr. Sulu, are you prepared to receive the access code?"

"Ready, Mr. Spock," Sulu said with a nervous chuckle. "Maybe between us, we can make *this* seventen split too."

Chapter Twenty-one

COMMANDER MONTGOMERY SCOTT straightened up from the tangle of wires spilling out of the back of the communications console and wiped the sweat from his forehead with the back of one hand while he tapped on the console frame with the other. With life support systems on non-computerized backup, temperatures everywhere were up three or four degrees, while here, in the service corridor that circled the bridge behind the consoles, it was up at least fifteen.

"That should do it, lass," he said. "Ye'll at least have power, even if ye' dinna' have the computer to sort through a few thousand frequencies."

"Thank you, Mr. Scott," Uhura's voice, muffled by the intervening mass of the console, came back.

"Good work, Scotty," Kirk said, peering in through the opening where the kickplate next to the turbolift had been removed. "Sanderson just reported in on the intercom, and he's making good progress on the impulse drive connections."

"Aye, Captain, but it's the warp drive that's goin' ta

take the time." He shook his head as he made his way along the access corridor and stepped out onto the oddly quiet bridge. All the sounds normally associated with the computer's neverending monitoring of virtually everything on the ship had been silent since Scott and a dozen of his men had simultaneously yanked its every primary and backup power cable. "Wi'out the computer to balance the antimatter—"

Suddenly, a hundred lights and displays came to life. Uhura's hand jerked back as if burned by the controls she had been using to manually make the settings that would eventually get her in touch with Starfleet Headquarters. The others tensed, their eyes darting from display to display, hoping to find some indication of what was happening.

Scott snatched his communicator from his belt as he darted back into the access corridor. "All posts, report in!"

By the time he had half circled the bridge and started down the gangway to the lower decks, the responses had told him where the trouble was. "Lieutenant Diaz," he said to one of the men he and the captain had standing by on every deck, "Mr. Claybourne on deck nineteen doesn't report in."

"On my way, Commander," a deep voice came back as Scott reached deck three and continued to race downward.

On the bridge Kirk could only watch helplessly as the displays continued to come to life. His earnest attempts to manually shut the computer off were meeting with no more success than his and Scotty's sham attempt earlier. Their only hope now was that Scott and his men could pinpoint the power connection that Carmody had obviously reestablished—and take it out a second time.

"Captain!" Ensign Sparer's voice from the helm rose above the rest. "The navigation system is coming back on line. Three minutes until it completes orientation and alignment. Phaser banks heading for full charge. No response to any controls."

"Keep trying, Ensign, everyone. Try anything and everything. If we don't find *something* that works, Spock and McCoy really *will* be dead!"

"Captain," Scott's voice, out of breath and half-obscured by the echoing clang of his boots on gangway steps, burst from Kirk's communicator, "Diaz reports Claybourne's area sealed off. He's taking his phaser ta the door. How much time do we have?"

"Two and a half minutes, Scotty, if we're lucky."

Without acknowledgment, the communicator went dead.

An instant later it crackled back into life. "Shanti, Captain. Communication from Lieutenant Sulu. I'm patching him through directly."

Static drowned out everything for a moment, and then Shanti's voice came in again. "Go ahead, Lieutenant."

"Captain!" Sulu's wire-taut voice came through instantly. "No time for explanations, do precisely as I say and—damn! Stand by, I'll be back if I can!"

And he was gone.

"Sulu! Shanti! What—"

The sound of grating metal spilled out of the communicator, and a moment later the *Enterprise* shuddered as *something* crashed against it, though without the sensors under their control, no one could know whether it was matter or energy.

Finney had guessed right, Sulu realized as the shuttlecraft came within range of the *Enterprise*. A second ship, filled with Klingon technology, hovered less than a kilometer below the starship. A limited-range transporter was just winding down, its destination somewhere inside the *Enterprise* secondary hull. Someone, either Carmody or the Klingon Kelgar, would be in there, trying to restore power to the computer so whoever stayed behind in the other ship could retake control.

His frustration mounted as he watched. He would never have time to get inside the *Enterprise* and deliver the access code to the captain. The shuttle-craft was already being pushed to its limits, not another iota of impulse power was available. He had no choice but to take a chance on the radio link with Shanti.

"Lieutenant Shanti," he said, activating the shuttlecraft transmitter, "put me through to the captain. No time to explain."

"Lieutenant Sulu?"

"Yes! Now put me through!"

"Yes, sir."

Decelerating at full power, Sulu watched the *Enterprise* grow to fill the shuttlecraft screen.

A burst of static came from the radio, and then: "Go ahead, Lieutenant."

"Captain! No time for explanations, do precisely as I say and—"

Sulu broke off sharply as on the shuttlecraft screen, he saw the Klingon ship begin to quickly reorient itself. Within seconds it would have its weapons bearing directly on him. "Damn! Stand by, I'll be back if I can!"

He obviously wouldn't have time to send the full access code, might not even have time to reach the *Enterprise,* definitely would not if he approached it with any semblance of caution. Swerving sharply upward and to the right, Sulu accelerated rather than decelerated. The other ship was below and ahead of the *Enterprise.* If he could go high enough, he might be able to make his final approach on a line that was hidden from the other ship by the secondary hull, but even that would give him only a few extra seconds. Now if Scotty's men had managed to get the doors even a *little* wider—

But they hadn't, Sulu could see on the screen. Shanti's shuttlecraft still sat anchored to the deck just inside the opening, an opening obviously no more than a few inches wider than the shuttlecraft.

Swerving again, Sulu was aimed directly at the opening. No time to warn Shanti to move. He would have to come in high, above the parked shuttlecraft.

The flash of phaser fire distracted him for an instant, but the beam was wide of the mark, the attacking ship just then being eclipsed by the *Enter-*

prise's secondary hull and apparently making no move to get the shuttlecraft back in its sights. But if it was trying to keep a lock on whoever had been transported to the *Enterprise,* Sulu realized with a surge of hope, it *couldn't* move, not without risking losing the lock and having to reacquire it, and if they were on as tight a schedule as he was—

Focussing entirely on the increasingly narrow-looking opening rushing toward him, Sulu reversed the impulse engine on full power as he nudged the shuttlecraft nose to the right a hair, then to the left and—

With a horrendous screech of metal on metal, far louder than when he had exited barely fifteen minutes earlier, he was through, the impulse engine throbbing as it did its best to stop what was in effect a shuttlecraft-sized missile. There was a bone-jarring thud as the runners hit the deck and bounced, another as they hit again and the shuttlecraft seemed, in this confined space, to be going even faster than outside.

A final grating crash came as the nose slammed into the rear wall of the hangar deck, throwing Sulu bruisingly against the controls. He could immediately hear air hissing out through a break somewhere in the shuttlecraft hull, but he didn't bother to search for it, barely even noted its existence.

Pulling in a deep breath, Sulu activated the emergency field effect suit at his belt as he got to his feet and punched the door release. The suit's faintly luminous halo cast a softening haze over everything, but it would give him the seconds he needed.

But the door—

He hit the release again, but it didn't move. Jammed! The whole frame of the shuttlecraft must have been warped by the impact!

Hitting the release a third time, he simultaneously slammed his shoulder against the door, putting all of his wiry strength into the effort.

And again.

This time the door gave with a scraping sound, and an instant later the pressure of the atmosphere inside the shuttlecraft took over the rest of the job, as the door literally popped halfway open and the rush of air almost knocked Sulu off his feet.

Catching himself, he hastily slid through the narrow opening and raced for the nearest door in the back wall of the hangar. If Scotty had been successful in sealing the doors manually instead of letting the computer do it, he would be able to override the seal from this airless side. If not—

Hitting the emergency override switch, he gripped the lever that popped out of the wall flush with the edge of the door. Pumping at the lever only until a narrow crack appeared, he released the lever and jammed his fingers into the narrow crack, now filled with a torrent of outrushing air.

But it wouldn't move! Even with all his strength, augmented by the adrenaline he could feel surging through him, it wouldn't move! He was going to have to—

Suddenly, a second pair of hands, also sheathed in the faint glow of a field effect suit, joined his—

Lieutenant Shanti! He hadn't heard her race across the hangar deck, but she was there, the tendons of her hands standing out as she joined her strength with his and—

With a metallic grating, the door lurched open another precious few inches.

While Shanti continued to strain at the door, Sulu, his uniform scraping and almost tearing, forced his way through.

Inside, leaving the air rushing through the opening, he raced to the nearest intercom.

Chapter Twenty-two

"ONE MINUTE until alignment is complete, Captain," Sparer reported from the helm. "Still no response to any control."

His mind racing, Kirk nodded his acknowledgment. A thousand solutions must have shot through his thoughts in the last two minutes, but every one depended on at least *some* part of the computer being under his control. The only remotely realistic chance was if Scotty or Lieutenant Diaz could break into the sealed-off portion of deck nineteen and tear loose the power connection that someone had obviously restored. Was it someone who had been on the ship all along? Or someone who had come on with Carmody but had *stayed* on board, biding his time until the critical moment?

"Through the first door," Diaz's rumble filtered through the communicators, "but there's at least one more before—"

"Captain!" Sulu's voice erupted onto the bridge, not from Kirk's communicator, but from the intercom system, one of the few systems that operated almost as well without the computer as with.

"Sulu?" Kirk shot back. "What—"

"No time, Captain," he interrupted, his voice knife-edge sharp, "no time! Enter the following sequence directly into the computer, no mistakes, no interruptions. Are you ready?"

Hesitating only a fraction of a second, Kirk spun toward the science station. "Do it, Mr. Pritchard. Go ahead, Mr. Sulu."

Instantly Sulu began, pausing only once when Pritchard fell momentarily behind his steady but rapid-fire delivery. On the viewscreen the approaching ship seemed more obviously defenseless with each passing second. Sparer continued to monitor the realignment of the navigation system, counting down silently, mouthing the numbers to Kirk. Other readouts showed that the phaser banks were fully charged and directed toward the oncoming ship, lacking only the lock-on and the order to fire that would come when the realignment was complete.

Kirk's communicator started to crackle to life, another message from either Diaz or Scott, but he hastily squelched the sound and turned away from the science station. He was about to whisper a delaying message into the communicator, when Sulu ended the transmission.

"That's it," he said, and then, the tension in his voice notching even higher, "Is anything happening?"

Without waiting for an answer, Sulu raced on: "Get the shields up, on minimum range! There's a Klingon ship only a few hundred meters below, or it was when I came in. It could be closer by now. It had just beamed someone into the *Enterprise* secondary hull and—"

"Captain!" Sparer's voice broke in sharply, even as her fingers darted across the helm controls. "We've got control! Firing command cancelled, shields coming—shields up, minimum extension!"

"Scotty! Mr. Diaz!" Kirk snapped into his communicator. "Don't disconnect! We're back in business!"

A whoosh of relief came back through the tiny speaker. "Aye, Captain, the doors just unsealed."

"Stay out for the moment, both of you. Whoever reconnected the computer may still be in there, and probably is dangerous."

"No, Captain," Pritchard broke in. "Sensors show a lifeform—a Klingon lifeform—just completing transport to the ship Mr. Sulu told us about."

"All right, Scotty, take a look, but be careful anyway."

"Aye, Captain."

"Klingon ship departing, Captain," Sparer reported, "full impulse power."

"Don't lose it, Ensign! Carmody has a lot of questions to answer."

"Aye-aye, Captain. Readying tractor beam."

"Does it have warp capability, Mr. Pritchard?"

"Unknown, Captain, but—" Pritchard broke off as new readings appeared. "Warp drive ship just leaving sensor range beyond Vancadia, making at least warp eight."

"Heading?"

"Toward the nearest border with the Klingon Empire."

"Raise any ships you can, Lieutenant Uhura," Kirk snapped. "If it can be intercepted in Federation territory—"

"Subspace signal being transmitted from vicinity of Klingon ship," Pritchard began, but broke off sharply, his fingers darting across the controls almost as proficiently as Spock's. "Antimatter generator in Carmody's ship being purposely overloaded, Captain. Going critical any moment."

Pritchard had barely finished the warning, when the fleeing ship vanished in a brilliant flare that sent the viewscreen into a total whiteout.

On the bridge, there was silence as the screen recovered and, finally, showed the dissipating cloud of particles that had been Carmody and his Klingon-manufactured ship.

"At a guess," Kirk said grimly, "I'd say they didn't want us to get our hands on Mr. Carmody."

At the hiss of the turbolift door, Kirk turned sharply from the viewscreen and Admiral Brady's weathered face. He couldn't keep a grin from erupting momentarily across his own face as Spock stepped smartly onto the bridge, followed by a scowling Dr. McCoy.

"It took you long enough to decide to let them beam us over from that—" McCoy broke off as he saw Brady's face on the screen.

"And I'm glad to see you too, Bones," Kirk said, getting control of the grin. "You know the admiral."

"Welcome back, Dr. McCoy, Commander Spock," Brady said and then went on hastily, a touch of apology in his voice, "I'm sure you realize the delay was necessary. Captain Kirk wanted to be absolutely certain that the computer was clean, that there were no surprises left in the circuits that monitor transporter operation."

"A logical precaution, Captain," Spock acknowledged when McCoy seemed at a loss for words. "But do not allow our arrival to interrupt the proceedings."

"Of course," Brady said, seeming momentarily disconcerted by the exchange. "As I was saying, we have found no trace of the Klingon ship. We assume it altered its course as soon as it was out of sensor range and managed to evade our search." He shook his head. "With only two ships in the area, it wouldn't have been hard to do."

"They undoubtedly had their escape well planned," Kirk said. Glancing at Spock and McCoy, he went on. "It looks as if they delayed their departure only until they were absolutely certain Carmody had failed. Delkondros and at least a dozen others who may or may not have been Klingons masquerading as humans vanished shortly after the surveillance ships were destroyed. We assume it was an evacuation. In any event, it's obvious the Klingons weren't planning to give Carmody a second chance any more than Carmody was going to give Finney one."

Brady nodded. "Even if he'd succeeded, I'd wager

they would have found a way to get rid of him. Since he was so ready to betray the Federation, how could they trust him not to betray the Empire?"

"You can say that again," McCoy spoke up. "According to Finney, Carmody was out for himself and no one else." The doctor snorted. "He fit right in with the Klingons. Thought their 'advancement-by-assassination' way of doing things was just dandy and wouldn't have hesitated a second to use it himself."

"Will we *ever* be able to understand the Klingons?" Brady asked rhetorically, shaking his head. "Or humans like Carmody, for that matter? But Jim, what are the chances that the Klingons took a copy of Finney's program with them?"

"I'd say it's virtually a certainty, Admiral, but I doubt that they'll ever try to use it. For one thing, they were undoubtedly listening in on everything that happened right up to the second they took off, so they know that we'll have protection against that or any similar program. But even if they do, we'll be ready for them, now that Finney's seen the error of his ways and will be giving Starfleet all the help he can in providing that protection, even while he's getting the therapy he needs."

Brady nodded heavily. "Security at our psychiatric facilities will be a bit tighter this time. One more thing, Jim, before you leave the Chyrellkan system—be sure that the truth of the situation gets thoroughly circulated on both worlds."

"That will not be a problem, Admiral," Spock volunteered. "While we were on the Vancadian ship waiting to be beamed aboard the *Enterprise,* Professor Rohgan and Councilman Tylmaurek offered to work with us. They are convinced that the people of both planets will be most susceptible to reason now that the Klingon involvement is ended."

"I'm sure they will be," McCoy put in. "Once they knew what was going on, everyone on that shuttle was ready to forgive and forget. And Professor Rohgan sounded like he was ready to start pushing for Federation membership the second he got back to Vancadia."

"Excellent, Dr. McCoy. Excellent work all around, Captain, Commander Spock. Keep us informed."

As Brady's image faded from the screen, Kirk turned again toward Spock and McCoy. "You two scared the *hell* out of me," he said with a faint approximation of the grin he had first greeted them with. "I would really appreciate it if you didn't do it again."

"We will endeavor to avoid a repetition of the incident," Spock said solemnly.

"I can't say I'd enjoy repeating it either," McCoy said, and then added with a shake of his head, "But you want to know what's *really* scary, Jim? That bunch had a good chance of pulling their little stunt off. They probably *would* have if they'd just *trusted* each other instead of stabbing each other in the back every chance they got."

"That is most unlikely, Doctor," Spock said, not looking up from the science station readouts he had turned to as the admiral had signed off.

"Oh, and what crystal ball tells you that, Spock?"

"It does not require a crystal ball, Doctor, or any of the other devices charlatans employ. It is simple logic. I am surprised you cannot see that."

"To you, solving a six-dimensional equation in your head is an exercise in simple logic, Spock. How about explaining for us mere humans who have trouble keeping just three dimensions straight?"

"As you wish, Doctor," Spock said, turning toward him. "It is merely that if people are inclined to trust other people, they generally have neither the desire nor the reason to develop such schemes in the first place."

McCoy snorted. "And if pigs had wings, they'd fly."

Spock minutely arched one eyebrow. "I assume that is one of your human aphorisms, Doctor, implying that humans as a species are not trustworthy?"

McCoy shrugged, his eyes flickering around at Kirk and Spock and the rest of the bridge crew. "I guess we're improving, Mr. Spock—at least here and there." His expression brightened. "Under your expert guidance, of course."

"It is gratifying to know that you finally acknowledge my contribution, Doctor," Spock said, returning his attention to the science station instruments.

Kirk laughed as he momentarily and unsuccessfully searched the Vulcan's face for a hint of a smile. "Ahead warp factor three, Mr. Sulu," he said. "Take us out of here."

STAR TREK ®
THE NEXT GENERATION ™
Technical Manual
Mike Okuda and Rick Sternbach

The technical advisors to the smash TV
hit series, STAR TREK: THE NEXT
GENERATION, take readers into the
incredible world they've created for the
show. Filled with blueprints, sketches
and line drawings, this book explains the
principles behind everything from the
transporter to the holodeck—and takes
an unprecedented look at the brand-
new U.S.S. *Enterprise* NCC 1701-D.

Coming in July From
Pocket Books

POCKET
B O O K S

THE EXPLOSIVE NEW

STAR TREK: ®

HARDCOVER

PROBE

by
Margaret Wander Bonanno

Pocket Books Hardcovers is proud to present PROBE, an epic length novel that continues the story of the movie STAR TREK IV.

PROBE reveals the secrets behind the mysterious probe that almost destroyed Earth—and whose reappearance now sends Captain Kirk, Mr. Spock, and their shipmates hurtling into unparalleled danger...and unsurpassed discovery.

The Romulan Praetor is dead, and with his passing, the Empire he ruled is in chaos. Now on a small planet in the heart of the Neutral Zone, representatives of the United Federation of Planets and the Empire have gathered to discuss initiating an era of true peace. But the talks are disrupted by a sudden defection—and as accusations of betrayal and treachery swirl around the conference table, news of the probe's reappearance in Romulan space arrives. And the *Enterprise* crew find themselves headed for a final confrontation with not only the probe—but the Romulan Empire.

Now Available In Hardcover
from Pocket Books

POCKET
B O O K S

106-01